MCFLUZIE
"TAKE IT TO THE GRAVE"

I0673697

T. R. STANLEY

MOVE OUT · PUBLISHING HOUSE

COPYRIGHT

Copyright © 2014 by T. R. STANLEY

ISBN-10: 0692410058
ISBN-13: 978-0692410059

See all of our books at:
www.Moveoutpublishing.com

CONTENTS

CONTENTS

FOREWORD
BY: DEVON STANLEY

Through our lives to this point, our reality is only on the experiences that we have gained through our lives. Most people make assumptions and decisions based off of the knowledge and experiences they have gained in the environment that they have come up in. It becomes easier to understand and explain the choices that people make when you are exposed to the decisions that a person makes in their environment. In another environment, their reality is only limited to the knowledge that they have gained from experiences in the environment in which they are exposed to. A few years back I came across, *"Plato's Allegory of a Cave,"* in which to me describes why people of all races and upbringings have a different perspective, or reality.

There are three phases in his writings which are inside of the cave, leaving the cave, and outside of the cave. The book starts with a conversation between (Plato's mentor) Socrates and (Plato's Brother) Glaucon. Socrates begins talking about four men prisoners that have been bound to a cave for their entire lives. They are strapped and seated with their heads facing the cave wall. On the cave walls are shadows of animals and people. The prisoners take turns guessing which shadows will come on the wall next, and they give the best guesser accolades on being able to guess the best. They hear sounds, but assume they are coming from the shadows on the wall. This is their reality, and is all they have ever known. Behind them is a fire pit and a wall, with men holding up wooden models of characters

1

that are being displayed on the cave wall as shadows. The cave is a place where most of us live. It is what we know, and the reality of the cave is how we go through life and make decisions.

Phase Two is described as, "Being led out of the cave." One of the prisoners is released and is able to see the fire, the wall, the men carrying the various figures, and is now exposed to a greater reality. At this point, all he has ever known has been destroyed by experiencing what has been going on behind him for so many years. He is then led and forced out of the cave by the man who released him. This phase is metaphoric of gaining knowledge, and being exposed to a greater reality. The thing about this phase is that even though the prisoner has gained more knowledge, he is still in the cave.

Phase Three is outside of the cave. In the writings, Socrates explained that the prisoner was exposed to the sun, the animals the birds, and the bees. At this point he has been exposed to greater knowledge and has a total different reality of his initial perception of the cave wall. The released prisoner felt obligated to return to the cave to let his fellow prisoners know that there was more to life than just the shadows they have seen on the wall. The new prisoner no longer felt satisfaction in the games they were playing, the shadows on the wall, and neither the accolades that were awarded by being the best guesser. The problem was there was resistance, and the prisoners did not understand the reality that the released prisoner had explained to them.

Although the prisoners were angry at the released prisoner for spreading this blasphemy, it is the obligation of the released prisoner in the future to try and expose the prisoners to the greater reality, even if his life depended on it. Through my explanation of, *"Plato's allegory of a cave,"* I task all readers to take the journey with the characters in this book Mcfluzie "Take it to the Grave." Understand the experiences to gain the knowledge from their perspective, in order to understand the reality that they live in. It takes an experience to gain knowledge and understand someone else's reality.

"MCFLUZIE"

TAKE IT TO THE GRAVE

MCFLUZIE-

Pronounced: /mick-flu-zee/

Function: noun/adjective/verb

1: used to acknowledge the surprise, disgust or utter disbelief of a person; action or thing

2: used to describe the reasons behind the emotions listed above

3: after using functions 1 and 2 there's nothing left to say but Mcfluzie itself

CHAPTER 1

SNITCH

"Amongst certain groups, being labeled a snitch is dishonorable and could result in serious consequences. No matter the circumstances, you are expected not to report crimes to the police and you certainly are never to become a witness even if you clearly see who did it."

"**M**y name is Detective Smitten and this is my partner Detective Baron. I would like to talk to you about the guns and drugs that we found in your truck."

As those words uttered across my brain I realized I should have listened to Bam. I was sitting face to face with the feds. The next words that came out of my mouth were, "Talk to my lawyer." I didn't have a lawyer nor could I afford one. I figured I heard people say it all the time in the movies maybe I can buy some time to think things over.

Detective Baron then spoke up and said, "I know it's real out here in these streets. We already know how you got the guns. I just want to know why so I can help you."

These dudes were trying to use reverse psychology and it almost got me for a second. I moved further into the table, leaned forward and said slowly, "I don't know how, I don't know why, I don't know anything."

Detective Baron remained calm and said, "They saying that all the drugs and guns that were found in your truck belong to you."

Immediately I said, "They who?"

As I asked the question Detective Smitten rose up from his seat with his face all red and said, "I'll let you think about it in a cell," then he exited the room.

Detective Baron leaned in towards me and whispered, "I'm trying to help you here; we blacks need to stick together." Detective Baron then stood up walked to the door and before he exited he said, "Let me help you."

This nigga just tried to pull the black power card. I done seen this shit all too well. That good cop versus bad cop shit ain't gonna work with me. After about five minutes they both returned with a honey bun and Pepsi that was placed in the middle of the table. I stared at the honey bun and Pepsi hungry as fuck but kept a serious look on my face.

"I know you hungry," said Detective Smitten.

I leaned back in my chair and breathed out a long breath. He was right I was hungry as shit, I haven't ate anything pretty much all day.

Detective Baron slid the honey bun to me, then walked up to me and placed the soda in front of me. "You need to eat something it's going to be a long night," he said. Not knowing when I would be able to eat again I grabbed it and started eating.

Detective Smitten said, "So, did Officer Eden deliver that message to you?"

I froze and thought to myself. I hope these niggas don't think that this food was supposed to get me to talk. I responded, "What the fuck is that supposed to mean?"

The room grew quiet. Detective Smitten started throwing names at me. "Do you know Rell? How about Bam? Indo? Do you know Scoops?"

I responded, "No."

"Do you know Biggs?"

"Yea I know him."

The detectives looked at one another as if I was going to give them the info on him that they been looking for. They asked, "How do you know Biggs?"

With a laugh I responded, "Who doesn't? Biggs is the number one running back in the state; I bet your daughters know him too."

Detective Smitten leaned in towards me with a serious look on his face and said, "Look, I'm going to be straight up with you. We found some things in your truck that's going to put you away for a long time."

I cut him off and said, "Look, whatever shit y'all planted or found in my truck the shit isn't mine check the prints; we can take a lie detector test the shit isn't mine."

Detective Baron then says, "Well your homeboys said otherwise, they told my partners that when you picked them up it was already in there."

Detective Smitten interrupted and began asking me questions. "How long have you known them?"

"Maybe three weeks."

"How y'all meet up?"

"We was tryna get up with some bitches until one of you doughnut eating niggas pulled us over for driving while black."

"Fuck it, you don't want to tell us shit? These dudes aren't your friends you about to take the rap for all this shit."

The detectives then got up and walked out. I'm staring at the walls in this dim cold ass room and all I can think about is how I got myself in this situation, what my parents were going to say, if my girl was gonna leave me, or the possibility of not ever getting out.

After about thirty minutes I heard a knock on the door. I see Detective Baron open the door. He pushed my nigga Snacks in the room. I made direct eye contact with Snacks and he gives me a look as if he was saying don't say shit.

In walks Detective Smitten and he says, "Oh Snacks, we brought you to the wrong room but maybe we will give you some soda and a honeybun and you will SNITCH like your boy Shrimp did."

I was furious, I looked at Snacks and said, "That's this fat nigga shit I ain't say a word."

Snacks looked at me and said, "Nigga you SNITCHING? YOU DEAD TO ME."

Detective Smitten escorted Snacks from the room. Detective Baron began to walk behind them. Before he closed the door he peaked his head in and said with a laugh, "So you snitching on your hood now?"

I was confused and cold as shit. I tucked my arms in my shirt to try to get warm. Hours went by, I didn't hear from nobody and I dozed off. I heard the click of the door and in came Detective Smitten.

Before I could say anything he says, "You free to go." As he escorts me out the room I see my shoes on the outside of the door, he told me to put them on. As we walk down the hallway I see similar doors like mine that had shoes in front of them too. I saw Snacks room, then Thomas, Squirrel, and Meech's.

As I'm walking by I get a glimpse of all their faces and they all looked back at me grilling me as if I snitched. We made it to the front office and since my truck got towed Detective Smitten offered to give me a ride home.

The whole ride to my crib was quiet. As we pulled up in my driveway Detective Smitten looks at me and says, "If I was you I would leave this state, these guys are known to commit some serious crimes and I believe they are coming for you for not taking the rap." I was shocked but was too tired and happy to be home that I just got out of the car went in the house and laid in the bed.

"Yurrrrrp, Yurrrrrrrrrrrrp, Bitch pick up." My Nextel chirp was going off, it was Bam.

I said to him, "What the fuck you want? A nigga just got home."

Bam said something that brought me to reality. "DON'T COME OUTSIDE TOMORROW, NIGGA YOU A SNITCH."

CHAPTER 2

INSTIGATOR

"Instigators are themselves bullies. They get a sense of power just as if they were the ones actually doing the bullying."

It's the First week of school and I'm a senior at Greenville High School. I'm dressed in my usual shirt, tie, slacks and some timbs. You may be asking yourself a kid in high school dressing up every day what's going on? Well, I was raised a Jehovah's Witness. I lived in one of the upscale neighborhoods in Virginia Beach, VA called Creeks Plantation.

People classified me in school as a rich kid or lame based on how I dressed and where I lived. I made a name for myself though. When I was in 10th grade I told everyone to call me, "Shrimp Daddy Pimp." Shrimp was my rap name I used to battle rap in lunch and I was pretty good at it.

11

I grew out of that phase but it's always that one nigga that always can't let shit go. "My Nigga Shrimp Daddy Mutha Fuckin Pimp." I said to myself damn, here go this instigating ass nigga Bam. You see Bam was a nigga that lived in an uppity neighborhood like me but had cousins that lived in Woodridge. Woodridge was section 8 housing and was the roughest neighborhood in Virginia Beach. Bam was the type of nigga that loved to fight and most of all loved to instigate them even more.

I said to Bam, "What's good nigga?"

"Nigga I heard Muhammad was looking for you. He said he was going to smack the shit out of you when he see you because you fuckin with his girl."

"Man fuck that nigga Muhammad, Lisa was throwing the pussy at me."

The next thing I know Bam left. I headed to my first block English class where I knew I would see Lisa. As the bell rung I was sitting at my desk next to Lisa and I asked her, "Yo, so you fuckin with that lame nigga Muhammad now?"

Lisa said with disgust, "Hell no, that nigga like 21 in 11th grade."

We laughed and made jokes about how ugly and dumb this nigga was throughout the whole class. I couldn't do nothing but admire how bad this chick was. Lisa didn't have much of an ass but her light skinned completion, freckles on her face, and red hair made her one of the baddest chicks in school.
Lisa claimed she was a virgin but I always use to say slick shit to her tryna get to her crib like, "Yo I know

12

your peoples don't get home until later let me come over and use the computer." She always told me to chill but today was different, she said I can ride her bus home with her but she doesn't know how I was going to get home. I thought to myself I'll walk home. I was finally about to get some pussy for the first time. As the bell rang I grabbed my books and started walking Lisa to her next class which was two halls over. I gave Lisa a hug and she walked in her class.

When I turned around all I saw was Bam, Muhammad and about thirty other niggas coming down the hall. I turned around like I ain't see them but it was too late, I made eye contact with Bam.

Bam says, "Yooooo, Shrimp, Cuh? Bro?" I kept walking and I heard him again, "Nigga you scared." I turned around and the whole crowd walked up.

Muhammad says, "Nigga you been fucking with my girl? I heard you telling niggas fuck me."

I'm thinking to myself that's what I told Bam. Muhammad and I started going back and forth talking shit then out of nowhere.

"THIS NIGGA FUCKED YO BITCH MUHAMMAD. YOU A BITCH IF YOU DON'T SMACK THIS NIGGA RIGHT NOW," said Bam.

The crowd responded, "ewwwwww."

Bam then says, "Shrimp this nigga says he gonna smack you so I say you smack his ass first OR YOU A BITCH."

Muhammad and I stood face to face and the crowd was yelling uncontrollably. *I'm thinking to myself where is the teachers, or better yet where the fuck is security?* Next thing I know Bam grabs my hand takes it and smacks Muhammad across the face with it.

Bam takes a step back in the crowd and says, "Damn Muhammad he stole yo ass," with a look of amazement on his face as if he was front row at a Tyson fight.

Before I could even blink I saw Muhammad's fist coming at me. He caught me on my left jaw. I threw a left hook back and missed. My instincts told me to grab him. He caught me one more time on the back of my head as I was reaching to grab him. I finally reached him and held on for dear life.

I charged him against the lockers, scooped him, cocked my fist back, hit him in the face and it felt as if Ray Lewis tackled me. It was Super Cop Johnson our schools resource officer. This nigga was known for tackling the shit out of niggas. He yoked me up off the ground and escorted me to the office.

On my way there I could hear Bam saying, "Them niggas fight like bitches," all while he was giving me a look that spelled you better not snitch on me. As I'm sitting in the office I'm thinking did I win? Am I gonna miss out on some pussy?

The principal Mr. White calls me in his office. "Mr. Griffin, explain to me what just happened."

"Muhammad ran up on me talking junk, he threatened to smack me, so I smacked him first then we started fighting." Now this was far from the truth but it

14

was either lie or snitch on Bam and be a victim every day in school.

Mr. White then went to explain that I'm in his house and I got to abide by his rules, the code of conduct bullshit, and how I should have got a teacher if I was threatened. There was no way I could have gotten my point across; this nigga knew there were no teachers in sight. I ended up getting suspended for five days. I spent the rest of this Friday in (ISS) IN SCHOOL SUSPENSION.

After the last bell of the day rung I headed out the building and here comes Lisa, "Oh my God are you ok? I heard about your fight."

I immediately switched the subject, "I'm cool, so you still gone let me use your computer?"

Are you sure you don't have to go home being that you got suspended?"

I knew she was right I should be headed home but said, "Naw, my peoples don't care about that shit." Any consequences were worth my first taste of some pussy.

We headed to her bus and sat down in the back. One of her friends named Kiki a ugly big bitch that looked like an overweight Morgan Freeman who was known to cock block asked me, "Where the hell you going?"

I said, "To my cousin house mind your own fucking business."

As the bus reached Lisa's stop we got off, I heard Kiki childish ass saying, "Now you know Lisssaaa, Now girl you know girl."

We both ignored her and headed to her house. As we entered the house I went and sat down on the couch in the living room.

Lisa said, "Let's go to my room the computer is in there and if my parents come home I can hide you."

"Cool I see you got it all planned out."

We get upstairs to her room and her walls were filled with Lil Wayne, JA rule, and B2k posters. I ignored it and sat down at her computer desk. I began surfing the internet looking at my Myspace just tryna act like I'm actually being productive.

"So what exactly are you using my computer for?"

I paused, "ummmmm," my throat clears, I said, "I had to check my messages on Myspace for this party this weekend."

She walks over sits on my lap and says, "Let me see what these other hoes are messaging you."

Little does she know my inbox was damned near empty. I had no hoes; I was a 12th grade virgin.

"Y'all niggas are so slick you prolly deleted everything."

She then got up and asked if I wanted something to drink and said she was thirsty. While she was down

16

stairs I laid on her bed positioning myself perfectly for when she walked back in. She came in and sat down on the bed beside me drinking her glass of soda.

I was quiet. Then out of nowhere she says, "So you telling niggas you fucked me huh?" I was in a daze. She kind of resembled Gabrielle Union a bit from the movie, "Deliver us from Eva." I snapped out of the daze after she said, "Boy is you listening to me?"

"Yea, Naw, that was Muhammad that's why I had to whoop his ass today."

"Everyone in school said you lost."

I laughed and said, "Well I guess you fuckin a loser huh?"

She leaned over and said, "Aww you need a hug."

As she leaned over to hug me I grabbed her ass. I felt uncomfortable but I had to make a move. She backs off of me and then leaned back in to kiss me.

Hoping I can get a little more out of her I said, "That's it?"

She paused for a second with a quick smile and leaned back in to kiss me again. I felt her tongue slip through my lips. I opened my mouth to do the same to her. A thought went through my head of my homeboy Stretch talking about using what he called the One – Two- Three steps on girls to smash.

From what he told me first the girl got to like you which was a given. Then Step One you got to start kissing her. Check. Then Step Two you start feeling on

17

her thighs and ass. Check. Now the last step is to start kissing on her neck, then to her breast, start sucking on her nipples and you in there. So I eased my way down to her neck and started kissing and sucking on it all while I moved one of my hands to her breast. She began to make noises. At that moment I knew I was in there.

I turned her over on her back and eased my way to her breast and started licking around her nipples. I began to suck on them and she starts moaning louder and louder. *I passed all three steps, what's next? What do I do?* Fuck it I went for the pants. I sat up reached down to her pants and started to unbuckle them. She leaned forward and started to take her bra off. I threw her jeans on the floor and began taking my pants off. Now I'm in my boxers and shirt and she is in nothing but a thong. I leaned over started kissing her again and she says, "Put a condom on."

I reached over on the floor grabbed my wallet and took a wrinkled up condom out of it. I had to of had this condom for ages it was so faded I couldn't even tell what brand it was. I had to of had this condom since my freshman year. I opened the wrapper sat on the side of the bed and put it on. This condom had no lubricant in it but I wasn't going to let that shit stop me. I got back on top of her. I started at her belly button kissing her stomach then back up to her breast and then began sucking on her nipples again.

She started moaning and saying, "Put it in." I was lost for words, I grabbed my dick with my right hand and tried to locate her pussy but couldn't. This is where my inexperience kicked in. I put my finger down there, felt it, and then tried to aim again. I knew I had one more shot or she would obviously know I didn't know what the hell I was doing. She reached her hand down and guides it in.

"Oh shit," I said. This shit was a drug. This was worth the fight with Muhammad. She's moaning while I started stroking slowly. She's making direct eye contact with me and I felt uncomfortable so I put my head down and started kissing on her neck and continued to go to work. It felt so good you couldn't tell me I wasn't smashing the baddest bitch in the world.

I started squeezing her ass and sucking her nipples while I was stroking. I didn't know what to do with myself. Then, "Booooom." I looked up and I saw this brown-skinned 50 cent looking nigga looking at me like he was ready to kill me.

"Dad," Lisa said.

Her Dad said, "Get the fuck out my house before I kill your ass, I'm calling the police."

I dove to the floor, threw my pants on, sprinted down stairs and out of the house. I continue to run for about five blocks until I was out of breath then started walking. My mind was racing. "Rinnnnnnng," I could hear my cellphone ring and felt it vibrate in my pocket. I looked its Lisa.

I answered, "Where do you live at boy? I want to have a talk with your parents."

I hung up, I knew I couldn't go home; I just got suspended for fighting, and got caught fucking in my girl house. I'm fucked, Mcfluzie.

19

CHAPTER 3

RUN AWAY

"Most kids run away from home because the endangerment component was physical, sexual abuse at home or fear of abuse upon return."

It's Friday night and everybody that is somebody is at Greenville High School football game. It's the first game of the year for us and the anticipation of going to the state championship this year is in the air. I walked up to the admissions gate real low key knowing I'm not allowed to be here because I just got suspended. I made it thru the gate after paying my $5. I saw Super Cop Johnson across the field and quickly avoided him by walking around the visitor's side.

I made it around to the home side and I heard Kiki's loud ass yelling with the crowd, "HAWKS, HAWKS, HAWKS, HAWKS."

I went to the top row trying to avoid being seen by anyone. I started thinking of what to do next and weighing my options. I knew that if I went home I had to face my parents and even worse Lisa's parents. The 4th quarter rolled around and I heard the crowd go wild and the announcer saying, " He's at the 30 the 20 the 10 Touchdowwwwn Hawks." It was Biggs 3rd rushing touchdown of the game. I could see Bam and Rico run up to him on the field and give him a chest bump in celebration of his touchdown. As the clock ticked down to three minutes everyone started making their way to the exits. It was a blowout and Greenville was winning 32-0.

On my way to the exit I see Stretch. Stretch was one of my closest friends. He was just like me in a sense. We both talked about always smashing hoes and all the girls we had but neither one of us was really living that life at least until today.

Stretch said, "Bro, why the fuck you fight Muhammad for man?"

"Man Bam instigated the whole shit I ain't want to fight. On a serious note, fuck all that nigga; I fucked that bitch Lisa today at her crib."

Stretch's face grew with amazement. "Nigga stop lying on yo dick."

I started explaining all the shit that went down to Stretch with a lot of exaggeration.

21

"I'm hitting the bitch she screaming, don't stop, don't stop then her Dad came."

After I said that Stretch eyebrows was at his forehead. Then I continued, "So I looked at her Dad and kept going."

"Nigga stop lying."

I paused for a minute and said, "Naw but foreal her Dad said he was going to kill me, I ran a 4.2 Forty out the house."

We both started busting out laughing.

"Shrimp you a dirty nigga, you got my home girl in some deep shit," said Kiki while walking up to us.

"Man that bitch threw it at me and with as many niggas that be running in and out of yo shit you ain't got room to talk."

Kiki had to get the last word in while she walked away, "That's why you got your ass whooped!"

On my way out a lot of people commented on the fight, some say I won, some say I lost, but I knew one thing I was no longer lame ass Shrimp. We started chillin outside the school waiting for the football players to come out the locker room. I'm walking around thinking of my next move. I saw all the Woodridge niggas grouped up and I figured I would get out of there.

"Shrimp come here," It was Rico. I walked over to him and the rest of the group he was with was looking at me like I was their next victim.

Rico reached out to dap me up, "I heard you fought Muhammad ass today, I can't stand that nigga."

"Nigga that shit was weak but Shrimp you still my nigga," said Bam.

They then continued to ask me if I was going to the party with them. I looked around and I seen nothing but a bunch of niggas that was up to no good. I couldn't say no, these were the most popular and hardest dudes in the school so I told them I would go. *Where were we going? What have I gotten myself into?*

We started walking away from the street and down the highway and I see a white boy probably early 20's.

I heard Bam say, "I got the first one."

The guy walked closer and closer, he gets to the front of the crowd and walks thru it.

"YEEEEEET, GET HIS ASS!!" That's all I heard as Bam connected with this guy's face. He was out cold. All I could see was about fifteen people stomping, punching, and kicking him. They were tumbling over each other trying to get a hit in. After a couple of minutes everyone started scattering like roaches.

"Give me yo shit nigga," Rico and Bam started running his pockets looking for anything that could be of use to them then they took off running. Everybody split up so I followed Rico and Bam. We made it to a park a couple of neighborhoods away and meet up with the rest of the group. *I was lost, I was wondering was that guy dead and why did Bam knock him out? My problems just got even worse.*

23

As everyone was laughing and talking about what they did, I realized that they whooped that white guy ass for no reason. He was just at the wrong place at the wrong time. This was an every weekend thing for them. Everyone started bragging about what they did.

"Damn Bam you almost broke that nigga face."

"Man I fucked my Jordan's up stomping that nigga out."

We started heading back towards Woodridge. When we got there I was nervous as shit, I've heard about all the shit that has happened out here and I'm here.

"Cuh? Who the fuck is you?" I see this dude in my face that I've never seen before.

Stuttering my words I say, "Shrimp."

He started walking towards me, "What you doing out my hood? You ain't from out here."

I was lost for words then Bam says, "That's my nigga don't fuck with him."

He still continued to stare me down and said, "I don't give a fuck cuh."

I was not built for this shit. I knew I had to get out of here fast. Midnight came around, Bam started dapping everyone up and says he is about to go home. I do the same and follow him out the front entrance of the neighborhood.

When we made it to the entrance Bam stops me and says with a serious face, "No matter what, do not come out here without me."

I said, "Ok, I got you," and we kept it moving.

I didn't want to know why? We made it to Bam's neighborhood and I told him I wasn't tryna go home and asked if I can I stay at his crib. Bam shrugged his shoulders like he didn't care. Bam's Dad did some secret service shit overseas so him, his brother Ortiz, and his older brother Charlie aka Wolf had the free crib all the time.

When we arrived to his house Bam gave me a pillow, some blankets, and told me I would be sleeping on the futon in his room. This nigga Bam was on the phone with hoes all night long. I wanted to ask him to put me on but I didn't want to sound thirsty. I ended up dozing off. I was awakened by the sounds of music and a strong odor of weed.

I sat up and all I could say was Mcfluzie. This nigga Muhammad was sitting right beside me.

I stood up quick and said, "Bam what the fuck?" Bam looked at me and started laughing. *Was I being set up?*

Bam slowly put his cup of Kool-Aid down and said, "I know one thing I'ma fuck both y'all up if you fight in my house."

Bam's Brother Wolf came in the room and said, "What the fuck are y'all pussies yelling for?"

Bam went on to explain the situation and Wolf went to go get his boxing gloves so that we could go outside and settle the score. We went outside in the backyard and laced up the gloves. Wolf was smoking a blunt with his friend OC, a skinny dark-skinned nigga with dreads. I see where Bam got it from because it seemed like every other word that came out of OC and Wolf mouth was Mcfluzie.

Wolf stood between Muhammad brought us together and said, "If y'all don't throw your hands you gotta see me." Wolf backed away and said, "Go."

I squared up with Muhammad and started swinging. He was catching me in the face but I was catching him as well. After about two minutes we were both bent over exhausted. Bam walked up to Muhammad and asked him for his gloves so that he could box me. I had already taken my gloves off but Bam insisted on boxing me. Bam was jumping up and down talking shit ready to go as I was still putting my gloves on. Bam walked up to me and stuck his gloves out to give me a pound.

I reached out touched his gloves and continued to finish tightening up my gloves. While punching my gloves together to make sure they were on it felt like I was hit by a baseball bat on my jaw. I fell straight to my ass. I tried to get up but fell back flat on my face. Everyone was laughing.

I could hear OC and Wolf saying repeatedly, "Protect yourself at all times." I rolled over on my back and sat up trying to get my thoughts together. Bam and Muhammad walked up to me and started to help me up but couldn't stop laughing. Once I was on my feet we walked inside and I sat down on the living room couch.

Bam looked at me and asked me if I was ok and as soon as I nodded my head yes they started bussing out laughing again.

I ended up staying the whole weekend. On Sunday morning when I woke up I realized eventually I had to face my parents. I dapped up everyone and headed home from Bam's house. When I made it home I opened the door and walked in the living room. I saw my Mom sitting on the couch. I expected her to be mad but she wasn't, she didn't say a word to me. I walked to my room closed the door and laid on the bed watching ESPN.

I woke up to the door bell ringing, I looked out my window tryna see who it was. I saw a silver Dodge truck in my driveway that looked familiar. Next thing I know I heard my Dad yell my name, "Christopher, come down here." My family calls me Chris and whenever my parents call me by Christopher it's never good. I walked down the steps into the living room and I had a look on my face like I seen a ghost it was Lisa, her Mom and Dad.

CHAPTER 4

HOUSE PARTIES

"House parties among teens can turn into fatalities if the wrong crowds mix."

I've been on punishment this whole week. No TV, I can't go outside, I wish I could go to school but I'm suspended. I tried getting in contact with Lisa but her parents got her on lockdown. When she gets out of school she has to go to her grandma house until her parents pick her up and on the weekends she's with her parents. I'm thinking I will never be able to smash her again. Friday rolls around and Bam hits me up on Myspace and ask me if I wanted to go to a house party on Saturday night.

I didn't know how I was going to get out the house but I knew I would find a way. I cleaned the whole house spotless upstairs, downstairs, and bathrooms. You name it I cleaned it hoping my parents would notice, and let me off the hook. I got Stretch to get his Mom to call mine so I could stay the night over his house. You see Stretch was far from a saint but my parents viewed him as a positive influence.

Now Stretch's sister was a whole different story. Her name was Carmen and she was as advertised. My nigga once told me that she kept a jar full of nut in her bedroom of all the niggas she smashed. I heard so much shit about Carmen, and I know Stretch did too but we never discussed it. Stretch and his Mom came and picked me up and we headed back to his house. I was hoping Carmen came because she had the fattest ass. We sat in his room for a while and tried to holla at every decent girl on Myspace that we could.

Stretch's Dad had a real nice camera so we would take real nice glamour shot type pictures with our shirts off to fool these girls on Myspace. Later that day I got a call from Bam he told me to meet him out Woodridge at 8pm. Stretch was completely against this. He pleaded with me to stay and told me that Bam and the others were up to no good.

Nothing could stop me from going. I got dressed and headed out to meet Bam. When I got out there it was about thirty people all in white tees standing outside smoking weed. A guy named Justin walks up to me and asked me if I wanted to hit the blunt. I knew I couldn't say no so I put it in my mouth, puffed my cheeks up, and blew out smoke. I wasn't sure if everyone around me was aware that I didn't inhale but nobody said a word.

Bam then came up to me and asked me to come with him to get Rico. I followed him. When we made it to Rico's house a tall dark skinned guy opened the door, "What's good Bam? Who is this nigga?" Bam then continued to explain that I was his homeboy and everything was cool.

When we walked in I saw everyone in the living room sitting on the couch. It was me, Bam, Rico, the tall dark-skinned dude, two other dudes I never seen before and what appeared to be a kid who was about five years old. After everyone sat down Rico started rolling up some weed. After he finished he lit it up took three hits and passed it to the tall dark-skinned dude.

He took three hits and said, "Y'all wanna see some crazy shit?" He passed the blunt to the little kid; the kid puts it to his mouth and inhaled. *I was thinking to myself this is a damn kid, this is fucked up.* I look around the room and everyone is laughing at this kid smoking like a pro.

He then takes it from him and passes the blunt to me. I said, "Naw I'm good I smoked earlier."

Bam then said, "Nigga you was smoking that Reggie, this that Purple Haze nigga."

Fuck it. I put the blunt to my mouth, puffed my cheeks, and blew smoke out. I did this three times and then attempted to pass the blunt to the dude beside me.

"You chiefin ass nigga, you didn't even inhale that shit."

Rico caught me; he was a pro at this shit so he knew when someone was bullshiting. I put the blunt back to my mouth and inhaled again. I started coughing uncontrollably.

"Virgin lungs," was all I could hear from Rico as I was coughing. He kept repeating it, and repeating it.

Bam said, "Hit that shit again!"

I took two more hits; I didn't feel a damn thang. The blunt made its way around the circle and back to me again. I took three more hits and passed it while coughing occasionally. When the blunt made it back around to me the third time I looked up and noticed that everybody in the circle had a blunt in their hand.

I thought I only hit the blunt six times when really I was hitting six different blunts.

I said, "I'm high as a bitch." I don't know why I said that but that's all that came to mind. I began getting dizzy. Everyone around me was dying laughing. My legs felt numb and I'm saying, "I can't feel my legs, I can't feel my legs."

Rico continued to egg shit on, "Yo Shrimp yo Dad just called, he outside."

I looked around scared and said, "Huh? No, hide me. Tell him I ain't here."

They continued to laugh. I was on cloud nine. I was lost, confused, and I heard Rico repeating, "Virgin lungs, Virgin lungs."

Finally, Bam told me to go outside and get a fresh breath of air. I stood up and it felt as if I was floating. I walked outside and sat on the stairs. I started to get myself together.

Bam came out shortly and said, "Nigga you straight?"

I told him everything was cool and we headed to meet up with the rest of the group. After we all met up we started to walk to the party. We were about thirty five deep all in white tees. As we are walking everyone started joking each other. I was in another world.

Justin says, "Shrimp you a ollllllll short ugly ass, Gary Coleman looking ass nigga."

Justin had on red jeans and a long white tee I replied, "Nigga it look like you had your period in your jeans. Nigga give Eddie Murphy his pants from Delirious back. Nigga you look like a handmade Pokémon." I was on fire everyone was rolling Justin himself was laughing. This weed made me the funniest nigga in America.

We made it to the party, rang the doorbell, and this bad bitch named Tiffany answered. Tiffany reminded me of Jada Pickett Smith with her perfect light skinned complexion, and petite frame.

Next thing I know Bam and Rico raced past her yelling, "Nigga Woodridge in the building, Nigga Da Clique in the building." Da Clique was a neighborhood gang that everyone in Woodridge and some other hoods were a part of. Everyone in Da Clique was jumping around thru the party getting hyped. People in the party were moving out their way as if they didn't want any problems. After we all entered the party we posted up on the wall. I felt like I was Alpo. I felt untouchable.

Girls were bent over grinding on dudes. I never saw this before but on TV. I was standing right next to Bam and a girl walks by. Bam grabs her arm she turns around and gives him a strange look.

"Fuck you bitch nobody want that whack shit anyway," said Bam.

Bam leant over and said to me, "Man I don't know about you but I'ma get my meat rode tonight."

Another girl walked by and he pulls at her, this time she walks up to him turns around and starts grinding on him, "Ayyyyyyyyyyye," that's all Bam was saying in amazement as he looked at her ass.

The girl then grabbed his hands, puts them up in the air, and starts grinding even harder. Bam then pushes her back down and she touches the floor. I looked across the party and I saw Rico was lying on the ground. He had a bad Carmel chick with micro braids on top of him grinding. I had to find me a bitch and I had to do it quick. I saw a girl standing in front of me dancing. *Was this a sign? Was she inviting me to come dance? What do I do?* Fuck it I walked up on her and brushed up against her ass, she looked back at me with a hard stare. I pulled on her arm and said, "Can I get a dance?"

She backs up, bends over and begins to grind on me. She was throwing it hard and I was starting to take a step back, then another one, and another one, and out of nowhere I heard someone talking in my ear. It was Bam.

"Damn Shrimp that bitch throwing it." He puts his hands on my back and holds me up. Once I had the

33

support I did what Bam did. I pushed her back down and she touched the floor.

"Got Damn," I said as I was leant back watching her grind on me.

Justin walked up and I could hear him behind me say, "Don't let that bitch break you nigga tag me in."

When the song went off she stopped, I had to get this bitch number any chick that can do that I needed her on my team.

She began to walk off, I walked up to her and asked her what her name was, "Tiffany," she replied. This was the same bad chick that answered the door. I started running game.

"So do you have a man? I would hate to have to fuck yo boyfriend up in here because he sees me talking to you."

"No, I'm as single as can be."

"Can I get your number so we can finish this conversation later?"

"Yea, why not?"

I handed her my phone, she put her number in and then called my phone.

Bam walks up behind me and says, "You a sucka for love ass nigga, you need to stop lovin these hoes." This nigga Bam was truly a hating ass nigga. I worked for mine he should have worked for his.

Out of nowhere Justin walks up to us and says, "Yo, There goes that nigga CJ from The Ridge."

Now The Ridge was a neighborhood that Woodridge has problems with. Anytime they see each other it goes down. The dude CJ was with two other dudes. They were definitely paying these hoes all the attention and had their guard down. It was about to go down. As if things couldn't get any worse in came Biggs and some of his niggas.

The word starts traveling around amongst all The Clique niggas in the party that we was about to get CJ. Everybody started to get in position and surrounded him. Biggs walks up beside him and was chillin on the wall. I'm thinking ok they ain't bout to do shit, then Biggs swings on CJ and catches him dead in the jaw. CJ falls and his homeboys try to run. Bam, Justin, and Rico catch them. CJ and his boys were on the ground. Everybody that we came with started stomping these dudes out chairs was flying and everyone was running for the exits.

Everyone eventually scattered and we made it outside. Sirens were going off and we all took off running. The police must of knew that we couldn't act civilized because they responded too quick. We hit the next block and a police car spotted us. I was running for dear life I couldn't get in anymore trouble.

We hopped a couple fences; I heard dogs chasing us and the cops yelling, "Stop, I'll shoot." The fatigue was starting to kick in. We hopped one more fence, came to a major intersection and we all split up. I saw a 7eleven, ran inside, and saw Bam and Rico, "Act like you buying shit and let's walk to Bam house."

As we came out the store an officer pulled up, "Where are you guys coming from?"

Bam says, "Sir, we ran out of Kool-Aid at home so we walked to the store to get some Arizona's."

"Ok, you kids should get home its after curfew."

Everyone said, "Yes sir," and kept it moving. These niggas was hardened criminals. I could tell that this was normal procedure to them. We walked down the street, split up at Bam's house, and I headed back to Stretch's house.

When I walked in the room Stretch had a million things to say, "What the fuck nigga? I had to cover for yo ass when your Mom called. Why you ain't answering her phone calls pussy?"

I ignored every word coming out his mouth. I was traumatized. I was in a brawl, I'm high as shit, I got a bad bitch number, and I just ran from the police. I lay down on the bed going thru my phone as I listened to Stretch bitch about what could have happened. I go to my call log and I see Tiffany's name. I hit send and put the phone on speaker phone.

She answers, "Hello."

I said, "Hello, you know who this is?"

"Yea, Shrimp."

"I was calling to make sure you made it home safe."

As I said that Stretch sat up in the bed and said, "Who is that?"

Tiffany then continues to say, "I'm home safe but I should be asking you that. You and your Clique friends were fighting."

"Yea, some nigga from The Ridge was talking shit so we had to fuck him up."

"He was talking a lot of shit?"

"Well, Miss Tiffany I'ma let you get your beauty sleep, I'ma call you in the morning," I said.

She laughed and said, "ok goodnight," then hung up the phone.

Stretch's eyes almost busted out his sockets. He sat up on the bed slowly trying to digest what he just heard.

"Nigga."

"What?"

"Nigga is that Tiffany Yates?"

I lay back on the bed with a smile on my face and said, "I'm no longer a lame nigga like you Stretch, I get bitches."

We both started laughing. Stretch didn't like the new Shrimp but he knew as long as I got bitches that he would too.

CHAPTER 5

JUMPOFFS

"About 1 in 3 women will be sexually assaulted at some point in their lives, and it most often happens before the girl turns 18. Young females have an intense desire and need for male love/approval. It can be the result of sexual abuse or because the father isn't emotionally or physically there."

When I returned back to school I felt like a different person. People who would never in a million years speak to me are now holding conversations with me. My relationship with Lisa is over in my eyes, I'm now on Tiffany. I knew for me to smash I had to step my game up. I couldn't wear anymore dress shirts and slacks or hang with lame niggas. I now represented The Clique. I knew nobody would mess with me because who I was now affiliated with.

"What's up ain't you gonna walk me to my class," said Tiffany. She handed me her books and we continued to walk down the hallway to her class. While walking and talking with Tiffany I felt the weirdest thing, it felt like someone was staring at me. It was everybody. I went from being lame as Shrimp to walking with one of the baddest chicks in the school. *What does she see in me?*

Being at the bottom of the food chain in high school leaves you blind to a lot of things. Right before I went to hand Tiffany over her books in front of her class Bam walks up.

"I see you Shrimp."

"What the fuck you talking about Cuh?"

"So you go with Tiffany?"

Before I could even respond Tiffany says, "We just friends."

Bam paused for a second and said, "Friends with benefits?"

Tiffany ignored him. I proceeded to hand Tiffany her books, she gave me a hug and then went into her classroom.

"You better stop loving these hoes cuhh," said Bam. I asked him what he meant by that but he just kept saying, "Stop lovin em."

Later that day in lunch I ran into Stretch, "Bro I just talked to Tiffany home girl Erica." *I'm thinking to myself this nigga is tryna throw himself a pass off my success.* Stretch figured that if he talked to Tiffany's best friend about me that it will give them something in common. Stretch was hoping I would tell Tiffany he was feeling her friend and she would hook them up.

As Stretch was going on and on about his conversion he and Erica had about me I said, "Fuck all that nigga, you think you slick."

"How am I slick?"

"Nigga you tryna get me to tell Tiffany to hook you up."

"Nigga I threw myself the pass. I'm chillin with her today."

I couldn't let dis nigga Stretch reap my benefits. I'm the nigga that bagged Tiffany. If it won't for me he would have never been chillin with Erica. I didn't wanna sound like a hater, besides I'm the one who lost his virginity this nigga still a virgin. I had to challenge him, there was no way I could let Stretch win.

"I bet I fuck before you." I really pulled this nigga card; he had a confused look on his face. Then I said with a big laugh, "What you just gonna play fucking cards and watch TV?"

"Alright nigga bet $50."

"Bet Nigga!" We shook on it; I knew I had to go to work.

40

When I got home from school that day I called Tiffany, I didn't get a chance to say one word.

"So, yo boy Stretch feeling my home girl Erica I see."

I paused for a second thinking of a way to play it off and said, "I guess so." The phone was quiet, "So what you like to do," I said.

"I like to talk on the phone and go to the mall."

"Do you watch sports?"

She responded, "yeaaaaa." She seemed aggravated.

I continued to ask her another question, "You got any brothers or sisters?"

She got angry and said, "Why you gotta ask all these damn questions?"

"Damn, I'm just tryna get to know you."

She got loud and said, "All you need to know is my name is Tiffany Sereana Wilson."

I knew where she was going with this and I fucked up. I had to test her to see if she really about that life.

I said, "Tiffany when you gone stop bullshitting and let me smash?"

"What you say?"

"I'm tryna fuck what's good?"

41

She got quiet for a moment then finally said, "You ain't ready for this."

I got a response out of her, I knew it was over so I began to ask her when she was tryna chill. She said she wanted to go to the movies so we set it up for that Friday. I was in there but there was only one thing, I wasn't about to take the bus to the movies. Later that day when my Dad got home I asked him could I drive his old Explorer to the movies with Stretch. I had my license and he let me drive it from time to time to get groceries or go to Stretch's house. He said it depends on how I did that week in school. I didn't care what anyone said to me that whole week I was not gonna get in trouble. I had an opportunity to smash a bad chick.

Something was strange; I ain't heard from Stretch in a while. I called him no answer, his phone was going straight to voicemail. I called Tiffany back that night and we talked for hours about what we were going to do to each other. I told her my Dad was gone let me use his truck to go to the movies and she asked if I wanted Stretch and Erica to come along. I made a joke out of it and said, "Naw don't get scared now you talked all that shit you gotta live it now." She laughed and we ended up talking all night until we fell asleep with each other on the phone.

The next morning in school I saw Stretch, "Yo nigga I been calling yo ass all yesterday."

Stretch started looking into space and said, "Word."

I then started to ask him what happened between him and Erica. He tried to play stupid so I kept asking

42

him. "Nigga did you fuck or not ye or ne?" No answer, I knew I had to say some disrespectful shit to get this nigga to talk. I laughed and said, "I guess you gone owe me double because I'ma smash both of them."

"Nigga, I smashed but don't say shit she doesn't want anybody to know."

I busted out laughing, "Either you lying on yo dick or that bitch a Jumpoff."

"Nigga why she gotta be a jump, how you know my game ain't that real? Pay me my $50 and don't flake."

Me being a sore ass loser I said, "I gotta hear it from her."

"Nigga I just told you she doesn't want anybody to know. When we meet up with them on Saturday I'll smash right in front of both y'all."

I'm thinking to myself this bitch Erica must really be bout that life if he gone smash in front of me. I must have picked the wrong one. I said, "Bet, double or nothing." I was setting up the ultimate flake, if I lost I wasn't gonna pay up. Friday afternoon came around and I'm sitting downstairs on the couch waiting for my Dad to come home. When he pulls up in the driveway I jumped up ran in the kitchen and acted like I was cleaning.

"Hey Dad how was your day at work?"

"Who told you to clean up?"

"Nobody, I just thought I would help Mom out."

I finished cleaning the kitchen then headed up to my room.

I lay down on my bed listening to music through my headphones but I had it low enough to hear every movement in the house.

After about two hours my Dad comes in and says, "So where are you going with my truck?"

I told him I was going to the movies and asked if I could spend the night over Stretch's house because I was going to go to the mall with him and his family on Saturday afternoon. My Dad seemed cool about it. He gave me a pep talk about becoming an adult and being responsible and to be home Sunday morning. When he left the room I called Tiffany and told her I would pick her up down the street at the 7eleven by her house.

When Tiffany got in the car she started acting shy so I started the conversion off about Erica and Stretch. "Now you know that nigga was a virgin right?" We both laughed all the way to the movies. She started telling me how Erica is her girl and all but she gets down. I'm thinking Stretch is one lucky nigga.

We get to the movies, I asked for two tickets to the 7:45 show and we proceeded inside.

"I'm hungry," she said.

I knew she was gonna say this shit. I asked her what she wanted and I went and got her a popcorn kid's meal like she wanted while she went and got us some good seats. After paying I headed to the theater, she was sitting all the way in the back, I handed her the food and sat down.

After she finished her food she caught me off guard and said, "Give me a kiss." I leaned in and kissed her. She had some soft lips and I could taste the strawberry flavored lip gloss she had on. Throughout the rest of the movie she kept feeling on my leg. I couldn't concentrate the whole movie; she kept getting closer and closer to my dick. Finally she reaches over and grabs my dick through the outside of my jeans.

I looked at her and said, "Yea you ain't ready." She started blushing and I said, "I'm serious."

When the movie was over we headed to the car and I was about to take her home. "I don't wanna go home let's find someplace to chill," she said. We drove around and around till finally I saw a Dicks Sporting Good parking garage. I drove in and parked on the first level in the back. We sat in the truck for a while listening to music and talking about the movie.

"Let me feel those soft lips again," I said.

She smiles and leans in to kiss me just like in the movies except this time when I leaned back her hand was on my dick. "I wanna see how big it really is," she said. She began caressing my dick through my jeans and then she unzips my zipper. She then pulls it out and starts to caress it again.

I'm thinking does she think it's big or small? She then began to start beating it slowly. I was waiting to hear her say something anything. "So I see you ain't scared," I said.

"I'm real about mines," she leans in to kiss me then dropped her head and started licking my dick. At

45

this point I am motionless, she then puts it in her mouth and starts stroking it slowly up and down.

"Ohhh Shiiiit," was all I could say. She continued for a few more minutes and stopped, "Why you stop for?"

"You ain't ready for all of me."

Now was not the time for games she had to continue. I saw the look on her face and she was dead serious. I didn't know what blue balls felt like but at that point it felt like my nuts weighed a ton. I tried to fight the pain and remain calm. I zipped my pants back up backed out the garage and headed to take Tiffany home.

We had a little small talk on the way but nothing that was going to lead to her finishing the job. When we reached 7eleven I gave her a kiss, a hug, and we parted ways. I made it to Stretch's house around 11:30pm and he still wasn't home yet. I parked in front his house until he got there. I heard a knock on the window. "Wake yo scary ass up," it was Stretch at 3 o'clock in the morning.

I opened the door, followed him into the house, and into his room. For some reason I couldn't sleep; I had the late night munchies. I got up off the futon and headed over to the kitchen. As I walk thru the living room I saw Carmen lying down on the couch watching TV. I said to Carmen, "Carry yo ass to sleep and put some damn clothes on."

Carmen laughed and said, "You ain't my daddy or my mommy." She had on some tight booty shorts that looked like they were Stretch's gym shorts in 3rd grade.

I grabbed a Capri Sun out the refrigerator and a Pop Tart out of the cabinet. I went into the living room where Carmen was and said, "Move yo ass over so I can sit down."

"Boy why you in here? Why you can't eat that shit in the room?"

I looked at Carmen and explained to her that I didn't wanna wake up Stretch because sipping that Capri Sun would be loud. Carmen started laughing but still didn't move. I grabbed her leg and she tried to kick me. I said, "If you don't move I'ma lay on top of you."

I took a big bite of my Pop Tart and a long sip of my Capri Sun and then laid on Carmen's back. After I lay down she slid forward and I was now positioned behind her on the couch. I said in a joking manner, "So can you move now?"

Carmen was quiet for a second and said, "You know you like this."

With those words and the fact that I was looking at her ass anyway my dick got hard as a rock. As soon as Carmen felt it she slid her ass back up against my dick and started grinding on it. I was lost for words; this was my best friend's sister. I reached around and started feeling on her breasts; she had on no bra so I went inside her shirt and started caressing her breasts.

Carmen reached her hand behind her and grabbed my dick as if she was about to slide it in raw daddy. I started to sit up on my knees and she was bending over. I was about to wear this donkey ass out. I got in place behind her and pulled her shorts down. I

47

rubbed my hand on her pussy and the next thing I know she jumped up.

I was so much in the zone that I wasn't paying attention to my surroundings. I heard the footsteps that made her jump up and they were close. I had no other option. I quickly pulled my shorts up, dove flat down on the couch and played sleep.

Stretch walked in the living room and tapped me on my back, "Get up bro, and go in the room."

I played it off like I was sleep and started walking towards the room.

Before I made it out the living room I heard Carmen say, "I told his ugly ass to get up. He drinking up all the Capri Suns and shit."

This bitch sold it better than David Blaine. I made it to the room jumped on the futon and was knocked out. I woke up to the smell of Dove soap and 50 cent playing on Stretch's computer.

"Wake yo ass up nigga we got a double date and my bitch want round three," said Stretch.

I hopped up and hit the shower then the kitchen to get something to eat. When I took my phone off the charger it was 8:37pm. I had slept the whole day away.

"No need to call Tiffany she with Erica." This nigga Stretch has become a thirsty nigga.

We headed out the house to go pick Erica and Tiffany up and I asked Stretch, "Is we driving your Dad car or am I driving mine?"

48

"We ridin separate you ain't about to cockblock on me nigga."

I followed Stretch to Erica's house where we picked up Erica and Tiffany. They come out the house with these skirts on both of them looking good as hell. We decide to find a spot to chill and just hang out. I told Stretch to follow me. We headed to the Dicks Sporting Good parking lot. I knew we would be here for a while and I didn't want anybody riding up on us so I went all the way to the rooftop.

Stretch and I parked about ten spaces away from each other. I saw Stretch get out and was leaned up against his car with Erica tonging her down. I told Tiffany to get in the back seat with me. I lay the back seats down and we just lay there for a while talking about school and gossip shit. I then start kissing her and hit her with the 1-2-3 steps. I got her skirt off, started sucking on her nipples, and feeling her ass.

"Stop," We made eye contact and she said, "I don't usually do this, I just met you but I really like you."

"Me either but it's something special about you."

I believed her; she gave me the most innocent look in the world. I just knew I was the only nigga to make her give it up this quick. We both got completely naked. I continued to kiss her and I then reached for my pants to get a condom. When I glanced out the window to see what Stretch was doing he was on top of the car smashing Erica. *I'm thinking my nigga Stretch getting it in I had to do the same.*

I put the condom on and got on top of her. She tells me to lie down and gets on top. She slides my dick in and starts riding it. Fuck that I don't usually do this shit this bitch was a pro. She got up and laid on her stomach, I started hitting it from the back. She was moaning loud. I started hitting her harder and faster I wanted Stretch to hear this shit because I could damn sure hear Erica. I'm in a whole nother world she's screaming, "Faster, faster, faster."

I hear a knock on the window. I ignore it and keep going, then another knock. I stop and I can't see out the window because it's fogged up. I rubbed my hands on the window and I saw a white guy with uniform on and a flashlight. "Oh shit the police," I said.

Tiffany started screaming, "Oh my god, oh my god," as she's throwing her clothes on.

I put on my boxers, jeans and shirt then hopped out the truck. I thought this nigga Stretch left me and didn't even warn us.

"Shrimp you good," said Stretch.

"Yea, I'm straight."

The officer was a Rent A Cop he was the overnight security officer. "Ok, the party is over you got five minutes to get off this lot or I'm calling the cops."

I jumped back in the truck, Tiffany hopped in the passenger seat, and I raced out the garage behind Stretch. The Rent A Cop followed us about three blocks and hits a u turn. Stretch and I dropped Erica and Tiffany off, said our goodbyes and headed home to his house.

Stretch said, "I set that shit off, nigga where my $100?"

"Naw nigga I did."

We both agreed that neither one of us had to pay up it was the craziest night we ever had. We laughed and joked about it on the phone with our girls and amongst each other until we fell asleep.

Monday in breakfast at school I was sitting with Bam, Rico, Scoops, and the rest of the crew when Bam says, "Yo, Shrimp you a cuffin ass nigga man, I was hitting you up all weekend."

"I was with my girl."

Rico said, "Who your girl?"

Bam said, "Tiffany."

Everyone at the table started laughing. "Y'all some hating niggas," I said.

Bam said, "Naw foreal, she bad did you kiss her?"

"What nigga!? I did more than kiss her." The table got quiet. I kept on going, "Yea man me and Stretch had Tiffany and Erica on the rooftop this weekend."

Rico said, "Erica too and Stretch?"

"Yea Cuh."

Scoops says, "And y'all go with them?"

51

"Yea nigga," I was pumped. I said, "She told me I'm the first nigga she gave it up to that quick too nigga, I be putting in that work." Again silence.

Scoops said, "Man y'all some dirty niggas you ain't gon tell this man?"

"Tell me what?"

Bam said, "Man I told you not to love these hoes."

The whole table busted out laughing again. I said, "What's that supposed to mean nigga?"

Bam says, "She file and you wifed her."

"Huh?" I was confused.

Finally after a minute of tryna figure out what Bam meant Rico says, "Nigga we ran a train on Erica Stretch girl, and Tiffany yo girl, two weeks ago, they Some JUMPOFFS!"

CHAPTER 6

SOCIAL NETWORK

"Using Social Networks was a major stepping stone for people who were scared or shy to engage interest in the other sex."

As if things couldn't get any worse for me, my parents said that they wanted to sit down and have a family meeting. Usually when they say this I'm about to get some real good news or some bad news. "Christopher," my Mom called me. I came downstairs to see my parents sitting at the kitchen table with a folder filled with paper. My body started to feel hot as I walked to the table, pulled the chair out and sat down.

"Son I have some good news," said my Dad. I exhaled a long breath of relief. He then proceeded, "My job just gave me the promotion that I have been waiting for."

The room grew quiet, "You should be happy Chris, we are going to be moving to Pennsylvania," said my Mom.

"Pennsylvania? I can't move there, I have to finish my senior year."

"We have already made arrangements for you to attend a nice school up there, you will like it," said my Mom.

So many thoughts started racing through my mind. *I was popular here. Everyone knows Shrimp. I'm in Da Clique. They need me here.* My parents wouldn't understand that. There was no way I was going to let this happen. I had to think of something quick then I said, "Stretch's parents would let me stay with them to finish the school year out."

My Dad took a deep breath and said," I don't know Chris, that could be too much on his parents."

"Well if I get his parents to call you and say its ok then can I stay?"

My parents looked at each other then looked at me. "If they say its ok, and that's if," said my Dad. We continued to talk more about Pennsylvania and they started showing me pictures of the new house they were moving to. When we were all done I headed to Stretch's house.

"Cuh, my peoples moving to Pennsylvania."

"When? Stop lying nigga."

I explained to him the whole situation and told him what my parents said about staying with him.

"Man, you don't like to fuckin listen to people and my parents ain't having that shit."

"Nigga, I get good grades and plus we gonna be doing nothing but smashing these hoes and chillin."

Stretch seemed excited but there was something holding him back from his stamp of approval. I could see it all in his face I said, "So what's the problem."

"If you keep fucking with those niggas in Da Clique and doing that hot shit you can't stay here."

I assured him that it was just a phase and that I was focused just on school, getting a job and girls.

"I believe you man don't fuck me over." Stretch headed out the room, into his parents room, and explained my situation to them. I sat on his bed waiting to hear the verdict. About ten minutes later Stretch comes and tells me his parents wanted to talk to me. I got up off the bed and headed to his parents room; I started sweating bullets. I was pretty cool with his parents but these were about to be different circumstances, I was asking them to live there.

As I entered the room before I could even speak Stretch's Mom says, "So Chris your parents are moving and you wanna finish the school year here?"

"Yes maam."

Stretch's Dad interrupts, "Well, you know my son speaks highly of you and it seems like you are a good kid." Stretch's Dad then went on to talk about the terms and living arrangements. He said that I would have to find a job, pay $175 a month in rent and be respectful of myself and everyone else.

I felt like I was about to explode with joy. After my conversation with Stretch's parents we headed back to his room. "Nigga don't fuck this up for yourself," said Stretch.

"Man why would I disrespect your house or parents? Cuh, we go way back."

By this time Stretch's mind was already on to the next thing. Myspace. Stretch began talking about his ultimate plan. He felt that there was no reason to go to parties or to the mall to bag girls; he said it was all on Myspace. Now we have used Myspace in the past to try to bag chicks but Stretch had a formula now. Not only did we have the glamour shot type pictures but we now had game. Stretch would say something off the wall random to chicks like, "I bet that pussy good or I thought you were supposed to come over today?"

Stretch didn't use it as a pick line but more to get a females attention, and once he did get their attention it was over. I figured I would try it. When I got home that night I started looking for nothing but bad chicks and sending messages. I probably sent well over twenty five different messages. Finally I got a reply back. "What are you talking about?" It was a message from a girl named Temeaka.

I sent her a message saying, "So why you had to go around and tell people that?" I knew I had her. I responded to her by saying, "Wrong person but what's your name?"

She responded back with her name and I was in there like swimwear. I got her number and began talking to her on a daily basis with intentions to meet up. A couple of weeks went by and by this time I had already moved in with Stretch.

I had gotten a job at Food Lion and my Dad left me his truck before he left to Pennsylvania. I had probably over eight different girls I was talking to that I bagged on Myspace. I was really getting it, but one stood ahead of the rest. Temeaka. This chick was a freak. She liked to fantasize about having sex with rose pedals on the bed and floor, and me pouring candle wax on her. I had to set up an appointment with her ASAP.

We ended up meeting one Friday afternoon. I drove to her sister crib to pick her up. I remember seeing her and thinking she don't look as good as her Myspace picture but she was still bad. Temeaka reminded me a lot of LisaRaye, she had that raised eyebrow I'ma bad bitch look. She walks up to the truck, I get out to open the passenger side door for her and to get the official look of her ass. It was official her ass was fat to death.

After I closed the door for her and get back in the truck she says out of nowhere, "Damn you short as hell." I couldn't do nothing but laugh. "So where are we going," she said.

"I got a surprise for you."

This chick was loud as hell and aggressive on the phone, it seems like now she was scared to say a word. We pulled up to Stretch's house and I parked. Stretch's Dad was home but he was asleep just as I planned. I told her to put blindfolds on as I walked her into the house.

57

"Where are you taking me?"

"It's a surprise."

We made it to my bedroom door. I guided her in
my room, closed the door behind me and asked her,
"Are you ready?"

"Yesssss," I could hear the excitement in her
voice.

I removed the blindfold. All she could see was
rose pedals all over the floor that led to a heart on the
bed, candles lit all over the room, and she could hear the
sounds of Jagged Edge playing through my radio.

With a big smile I said, "So now tell me, what was
your greatest fantasy was again?"

She still stood there stunned. I walked up to her,
started kissing on her neck, and feeling on her breasts.
She started kissing me back all while we made our way
to my bed. I sat down while she still leant over kissing
me. She stopped, stood straight up, and started taking
off her shirt and her jeans. She now had on nothing but
her bra and panties. I quickly took off my shirt and jeans
and got all the way down to my boxers. She pushed me
back on the bed and pulled my dick out. She got down
on her knees and started sucking it; my eyes were to the
ceiling.

After about five minutes she rises up and takes
her bra and panties off. "Take those off," she says
talking about my boxers. I take them off and slide back
on the bed. She then sits on top of me and started
kissing me. She was real aggressive, "Smack my ass,"

she said. I started smacking and squeezing her ass while she was kissing and sucking on my neck. Out of nowhere she grabs my dick and slides it in her pussy.

I'm thinking what the fuck I don't have a condom on but it felt so good and wet. I didn't even bother to say a word or dare to stop it. The possibility of me getting her pregnant or catching something was completely out of my mind. She was on top riding me like a pro. I thought the previous chicks were good but this chick was in a world of her own. I felt myself about to cum about four minutes in. I tried to slow it down but she kept bouncing on my dick faster and harder.

I whispered to her, "I'm about to cum," she starts going even faster. I came inside her and she kept going. It felt so good I couldn't take it anymore; I tried to slow her down but still no luck.

She said, "Come on that's all you got?"

I grabbed her ass with both hands and started hitting it harder. By this time I done caught my second wind. We turned over; I got on top and started stroking while I had her legs up in the air. She's screaming all kinds of things out loud.

We were in the zone we went at it for hours. My phone started going off, we took a quick intermission as I leaned over to see who was blowing me up. I had twelve missed calls from Stretch in the past thirty minutes so I called him back.

Stretch started yelling, "Bro what the fuck man?"

"What happened?"

"Man you in there fucking that chick like a wild animal with the music all loud, fucking loud, and her screaming and shit got my parents mad as fuck."

Next thing I know I heard a knock on the door. Temeaka jumped under the covers. I walked to the door after I put my boxers on and opened it. Stretch busted in the room and says, "Man y'all hot as fuck Cuh." He then began to look around the room, it was a disaster. There were candle wax and rose petal stains all over the place. "Man my parents are going to fucking kill me."

"I'm going to clean it up."

Stretch snatches the covers off us and says, "No, clean the fuck up now nigga."

I knew there was no way I could clean this room up and drop her off before his parents woke up. I asked Stretch could he take her home while I clean up, and he told me I owe him gas money and get the shit cleaned up.

Stretch was already going out to see a chick. He didn't need the gas money but he always tries to take advantage of the situation. Me and Temeaka both put our clothes back on, I gave her a hug and a kiss, and she leaves with Stretch.

I slept all night until I had to be to work the next morning, and plus I didn't wanna have to run into Stretch's parents. When I got off of work I called Tameka. I knew she told me her sister had to work double shifts and would not be home until the next morning. I said, "Hey what you doing?"

"Nothing, I'm washing clothes and watching TV."

I could hear it in her voice that she was occupied but she kept saying she wasn't doing anything. We then got into a conversation about the previous night but she was real hesitant to talk about it. "Oh, so you must got you a new nigga over there now?" She got quiet. Jokingly I said," Tell yo new nigga I'm about to pull up in your driveway," and I started laughing. She didn't find it that funny. I said, "Why you so quiet?"

"Ummmmmmmm," and then she told on herself, "Stretch is over here."

"What the fuck is he doing over there? I'ma fuck both y'all up," I said yelling into the phone and then I hung up.

Little did they know I was right down the street foreal. I called Stretch's phone no answer, I called him again no answer. I started heading to Temeaka's house. So many thoughts were going through my mind. *Should I fight Stretch, should I smack this bitch, or should I try and fuck with one of Stretch's girls?* My mind was racing.

As I came up to her house I saw Stretch's car parked a little down the street. *I'm thinking this sneaky little bitch.* I parked behind his car and walked to her house. I knew they were going to be listening for my truck or the doorbell so I walked right in.

I tried to keep quiet and catch them in the act. When I entered the house I heard a noise upstairs. I creeped up the stairs and I noticed they were in the bathroom. I crawled up to the door laid down and listened. I could hear the shower water running.

"Man that nigga ain't gonna get here that quick you gonna let me fuck I just need five minutes."

"You are his best friend, and don't you have a girl?"

"Man Shrimp is playing you, he got a bunch of bitches, his real name ain't even Shrimp, its Christopher, see he lying to you."

This nigga was the ultimate cock block and hater. He actually took it this far. I was feeling bad for being about to cut his sister but now I have no remorse.

I got up and opened the door. I saw Stretch sitting on the toilet and Temeaka in the shower talking to him. "Man, Stretch you a bitch for this."

Stretch busted out laughing, "I knew you liked her, I just wanted to see if she was faithful."

Temeaka yells, "Get the fuck oouuutt."

We left the bathroom and headed downstairs to the living room. When we get to the living room we sat down on the couch and Stretch started telling me what happened. Stretch said last night when he dropped her off he asked to use her phone because his was dead. He called himself so he could get her number. This morning he called her and said he had to talk to her about me and it was serious. When he came over he said he tried to smash but she wasn't having it. She told him to leave and she went upstairs to take a shower. While she was in the shower he walks in and tried to talk her into smashing again and that's when I walked in.

I wasn't really mad at Stretch. We both were smashing so many Jumpoffs through Myspace that they all were fair game, but this particular attempted assassination hurt. I fulfilled this bitch deepest fantasy and this nigga Stretch again tried to reap my benefits. Later that day when we got back home we agreed that as long as we don't say anything about wifing a chick that she was fair game. I couldn't let this man Stretch try one of my bitches like that and sleep easy. I had to go after Erica.

I already had her number in my phone from hanging with her and Tiffany so I called her and just kept it 100. "I know you talked to Stretch and I talked to Tiffany but I'm really feeling you. This nigga Stretch ain't doing you right, he out here fucking other girls."

Little did I know I didn't need to pillow talk to get Erica nor did I need a social network. Erica responded back with, "I wanted you too. Tiffany think she all that and she can get anyone she want I'ma show her. When you tryna get up?"

I guess hoes are always gonna be hoes but this chick Erica I really had a thang for. Stretch gonna find out what goes around comes around.

CHAPTER 7

TURNING POINT

"Certain events in your life can cause a major Turning Point. Some can be for the good and some for the worst. How you live your life will truly determine the direction."

I'm leaving work; I got the windows down in my truck with the music loud listening to the radio. I drive past Woodbridge. "Yurrrrrrrrrrrp," I heard Bam signaling me to pull in the neighborhood. It's been a while since I kicked it with him out of school so I pulled in the neighborhood to see what he was up to. He was with his normal crew Rico, Slim, Black and Chubs. Bam said," Nigga where the fuck you been?"

"Man working and fucking these hoes you know."

We started talking about the gossip around school and in the neighborhood. It started to get dark. I said, "Ight, I'm about to head to the crib."

When I got back in my truck Bam walks up to my window and says, "Man roll with us to this party out Castlewood."

Now I knew two things. One I wasn't rolling with them because I have the truck they were rolling with me, and two Castlewood was an area where Woodridge had beef with. I said, "I don't know man I gotta be at work early in the morning."

Rico walks up and says, "Come on man it's gonna be mad hoes there."

Rico just said the magic words. I told them I would go to the crib, shower up, and meet them out the neighborhood at about 9 pm. I hopped in the truck, drove home and when I pull up I saw Stretch's car. I know this dude is gonna trip about me going to the party with Bam and them.

I walked in my room laid my clothes I'm wearing on the bed and hit the shower. When I came out I saw Stretch sitting on my bed, "Where you bout to go?"

I wasn't trying to hear the bullshit so I said, "I'm bout to go to this chick Ashley crib." I grabbed the clothes that I was wearing and took them in the bathroom with me to change. When I came back out I heard Stretch talking under his breath. I said, "Speak up nigga you talking low like a little bitch."

Stretch looked at me with a disgraced look on his face, "You said you wouldn't hang with those Clique niggas."

How the fuck did this nigga know? I said, "Man who told you I was?"

"Myspace. I'm not going to say a word, these niggas is just using yo dumb ass."

I'm thinking this dude is a page watching nigga. I wasn't trying to hear that shit I was trying to go out and have a good time. I finished getting dressed and headed out to meet Bam and them. When I got there I see Bam, Slim, Rico, Black, Chubs and they had four other niggas with them Jr, Rody, Rell, and Griff. Getting everyone in my truck was not the problem. I had already taken all the seats out in the back from when I was smashing chicks. The problem was I didn't know these other niggas like that, all I knew was they names.

Everyone hopped in my truck and dapped me up.

Jr said, "Yo cuh where yo damn seats at?" Everyone started laughing.

"I was smashing this bitch so I took them out and put a blowup bed down, I was too lazy to put my seats back in."

They started clowning me all the way to Castlewood. When we got close Rico called some girl he was talking to at the time and she gave us directions to the house.

When we got there I heard Chubs yelling, "The Clique is in the building get it up."

We made our way to the front door, rang the doorbell and nobody answered. We banged on the door and nobody came, so we made our way around to the back yard. We walked up to the back door and knocked, we could hear the music and people inside.

We kept knocking and nobody answered. Rody said, "Rico call yo girl nigga she bullshiting." Rico calls her and there was no answer. All of a sudden the music stops. Someone looks out the blinds at us and closes them.

Chub's walks up to the door and started banging still no answer. "Yo I'm bout to kick this shit in," said Chubs.

Bam and Chubs start banging on the door real hard then they started kicking the door. Still nobody answered the door. It was obvious now that whoever was inside didn't want us there. "Chubs on the count of three we gonna kick this shit off the hedges," said Bam. They count to three and kick the shit out the door knocking it off the hedges.

We all ran in the party yelling, "The Clique in the building."

It was complete silence. I heard the DJ say the party was over and everyone started walking out. I could see everyone I came with plotting on who to knock out. Out of nowhere I see Rico arguing with some Puerto Ricans and a black dude. By the time we all get to where Rico is they were in the car. The black dude was standing up on the passenger side with his arms on the door talking shit, "Y'all fucked my home girl party up y'all some bitches."

Rico kept telling him to get down from out the car and the black dude just kept talking shit. Everyone that rode with me started surrounding the car. The black dude then reached for a stick and pointed it at Rico saying that he would fuck him up. Rico wasn't saying a word he stood there angry as if flames were coming from his head.

Out of nowhere Rico runs up to him jumps, and punches the black dude in the face. As Rico lands he reaches for him and grabs him out the car. The black dude hit the ground and Rico started stomping him. Somehow the black guy makes it off the ground gets up and starts running. His Puerto Rican friends didn't even budge, they were about to witness their homeboy get an ass whopping.

Griff takes off after the black dude and walks him down. He catches him by the shirt. The black guy swings, Griff ducks and slams him. Before the black guy could even think about getting up we was on him. All of us started stomping him out. Bam and Rico started grabbing things out of the person yard we was in and throwing it on him.

I couldn't believe I was a part of this. I was actually stomping this guy too and I didn't even feel bad about it. "Shrimp go get the truck," said Bam.

I ran to the truck started it up and drove up to them; they were still beating his ass. They all hopped in except Rico and Bam these dudes could never get enough of fucking somebody up. Jr and Chubs hopped out and grabbed them, they hopped in the truck and we were out.

Rico's girl called him and you could hear it in her voice she was mad we ended the party. "Fuck you bitch if you would have answered the phone and let us in this shit wouldn't have happened." He hung up the phone and started bragging about how he fucked the black dude up.

We started hearing sirens so we took the back way out the neighborhood. I didn't know where the fuck I was going I just knew it would be away from the sirens. I came across a street that I was familiar with and it was a straight shot to Woodridge. We came up to the light and I heard Rico talking to someone in the car next to us, "What the fuck you looking at cuhhh?"

I couldn't see what was going on but I could hear it. "Those the motherfuckers that fucked JB up get the heat nigga," they said.

"Drive bitch they got a fucking gun," said Chubs.

I froze up I didn't know how to act. "Boooooom," the glass on the driver side shattered they threw something through the window. "What the fuck drive nigga," said Bam from the passenger seat.

The light was on red but I hit the gas and drove through it. The car beside us was a blue Honda Civic. I started going 55 mph and they still started following us. I hit 65 mph still they kept up. They pulled up right beside us; I could see in my mirror that they had sticks with knives at the end of them hanging out the window of their car. They were trying to flatten my tires; I started going faster doing about 70 mph.

Another car pulls up on my passenger side, "Boooooooooom," another window shattered on the

69

passenger side. I'm now doing 80 mph I'm coming up to a major intersection and the light was red Jr said, "Keep fucking driving they tryna kill us mannn."

Rell was infuriated with tears coming from his eyes in anger. He started screaming, "Fuck that shit nigga, fuck that shit, pull the fuck over. Shrimp, let me the fuck out, I'ma kill these niggas, stop the fucking car."

I ran the next red light and the two cars do as well. They were still throwing shit at my truck and tryna flatten my tires. *Where the fuck is the police when you need them we just ran two lights and there was nobody in sight.* I saw my life flash in front of my eyes. I sped up and started doing 90 mph and they were still on us tryna get us to crash.

I could hear Chubs on the phone with his older brother telling him what was happening. His brother told us to lure them in the neighborhood and he was gonna shoot their car up when they followed us in. We were about a minute from Woodridge. The Puerto Ricans was still chasing us; we ran another red light right in front of the neighborhood and pulled in. I couldn't tell if they were still behind us. I ran up the curb and into the parking lot.

I saw two guys hop out the bushes with guns in their hands; it was Chubs brother and his cousin. I could barely breathe. Rell was still going through a meltdown like Cuban Gooding Jr in *Boys in the Hood* did after Ricky died. We all started laughing but knew we came within an inch of our lives. *If I kept hanging with these dudes I would prolly end up dead or in jail. What was I to do?*

CHAPTER 8

HOMECOMING

"Homecoming in High School had festivities that you couldn't get any sleep waiting to attend. As always with those festivities come people looking for trouble."

It's Friday afternoon and we just got out of our prep rally. The whole school is hyped and can't wait until our Homecoming game vs Oak Valley our school rival. You see Oak Valleys football team was the worst in our district but when we played them it was live. From fights, to bad bitches, to watching our school run up the score, it was full excitement.

When school let out I had a plan. I was gonna chill with my niggas Rico, Bam, and Scoops after school in the cafeteria until it was time for them to get ready for the game, then I was gonna chill with Erica and get some head before the game started. What can I say life was good. I had a reputation around school for fucking niggas up, well assisting in doing so, and the hoes say my dick was big.

Those three things go a long way in high school. Your pride, your bitches, and the way you dressed are all you got. I had two of those pride and bitches. The way I dressed I faked it till I made it. A white, black, and red tee stayed in rotation. I had some forces I got from Stretch and some timbs I bought with my check from work that got me by. This is what everyone in school wore.

Mines wasn't named brand but who could tell the difference? As I'm walking to the cafeteria I see Stretch talking to Roshelle. I knew what he was trying to do. This man was trying to get some pre game head from the school football team jump off before the game. I saw that Stretch had left her alone and went to talk to Miss Anderson, his Math teacher.

I slid in quick, "What's good Rochelle? What you staying after school for?"

"I'm just chilin with my girls waiting for the game to start."

In other words she was staying after to get drafted by one of the football players. Now I wasn't a football player but I knew my game was way stronger than theirs. We began to walk and talk our way to the gym and met up with her friends Misha, Tawana, April, and Michelle.

We were sitting down on the bleachers watching the football team do a walk thru before the game. I received a text from Ericka saying her Mom just left to go to work and for me to come thru. I knew I had about a three hour window before her older brother got home so I proceeded to leave. On my way down the bleachers I heard April say, "You think you the shit?"

"Excuse me," Instantly, I knew I was dealing with a hater.

April then repeated, "You think you the shit because these hoes say yo dick is big?"

I laughed with a grin and said, "Well it is, the hoes ain't lying."

Out of nowhere I heard Michelle say, "Well let us be the judge."

Me being the cocky nigga I was said, "Ok," knowing that I wouldn't be able to pull it out in front of the whole gym. "I don't have a problem showing you but it's too many niggas around."

"Let's go in the classroom," says Tawana as I continued to walk down the bleachers.

I thought to myself Mcfluzie, this is one thirsty bitch. As I continued to walk they followed and we made our way to the health classroom. Michelle closed and locked the door behind us then Tawana says, "Pull that shit out I wanna see what the hype is about."

I reached down to unzip my pants and realized my dick was limp as a bitch. I said to April, "My shit ain't even hard."

"Rochelle get his dick hard," says Tawana

Now I knew Rochelle was a jump but I didn't think she would actually do it. Rochelle walks up to me, grabs my dick thru my pants, unzips it, pulls my dick out, and starts beating it. My shit was about 75% but I'll put my 75% up against a lot of niggas 100%. Rochelle continued to beat my shit. The rest of the bitches started walking up closer. You would think that this shit would make you horny as shit being around a room full of bitches with yo dick out. Wrong.

My shit could not get hard to save my life. "Y'all standing there help her get my shit hard," I said hoping they would join in. April started inching closer as if she was going to assist then, "boom," somebody was banging on the door. I put my dick back in my pants and sat down in the chair like everything was cool.

April goes and opens the door and in walks this nigga Stretch. "It smells like straight ass in here I knew y'all bitches went both ways." As Stretch made his way all the way in the classroom and past the girls he noticed me sitting in the back. I gave him this yeah nigga I took yo bitch again look. I couldn't help but smile at this nigga. Stretch looks around rubs his head and says, "Y'all in here fucking with a committed nigga y'all know he fuck with my leftovers."

Rochelle asks, "Who's your leftovers?"

"That hoe Erica."

The room got silent. I couldn't believe this nigga was hating like this. I walked out the room pass April and the rest of them and said, "I guess you a believer like the rest of these hoes," and laughed. I got out in the hallway and checked my phone; I had three missed calls from Erica.

I dialed her number and called her back no answer. I called again no answer. Finally she calls me back and says, "You rather hang with niggas then get pussy huh?" Before I could even say a word she hangs up. *Mcfluzie, I done fucked up the mission.*

I headed back into the classroom and listened to the conversation. Stretch was taking talley asking all the bitches if my dick was big or small. Now Stretch is like my brother from another mother but this nigga, when it comes to bitches it's every man for himself. All the bitches but one said my shit was big and Rochelle pleaded with her that my shit won't hard. "Rochelle let me holla at you," I said in a way like I had to really ask her a question. We walked out the classroom, down the hall, stopped and I said, "You tryna finish what we started?"

"Yea but where at?"

I lifted my keys up and said, "My truck."

We walked away quickly, I knew this nigga Stretch would cock block. We made our way to the student parking lot and into my truck. I drove to the back of the parking lot and parked. Before I could even put the car in park her hands was on my dick, she pulls it out and starts beating it.

75

I'm thinking this bitch better do something, I wasn't tryna have another blue balls epidemic. "Let's get in the back seat," she says. I opened the door with my dick hanging out, holding on to my pants, and quickly got in the back seat. After we both got in she reaches over grabs by dick looks both ways and begins sucking it. I sunk down in the seat. She said, "Are you looking out?"

"Yea, aint nobody out here girl."

I snapped out of the daze I was in and realized where I was. I was in the student parking lot. I had to be on the lookout. I seen a couple of people walk to their car but what stood out was what I seen from a distance. I saw a nigga walking from car to car like he was looking for someone. I paid it no mind. I continued to enjoy the services of Rochelle. I looked back up and the person was closer. *I said to myself is that fucking Stretch?*

It was but I won't bout to tell her to stop. I looked down and looked back up and he was gone. We were in the clear I sinked back into the seat put my hand on her head and closed my eyes. "Ding, ding, ding, ding," I heard the sound of my truck door open. This nigga Stretch hops in my truck turns the key and drives us off. I said, "What the fuck you doing nigga?"

Stretch looks back laughs and keeps driving. Rochelle had a look on her face like she couldn't believe it. We made it across the street from the school to the park and Stretch parks. "What's good am I next?"

"Hell no," says Rochelle.

"Shrimp I thought you told me to wait a couple of minutes and come out?"

Rochelle slaps me in the face, gets out the truck, slams the door, and starts walking towards the school.

Stretch starts driving beside her, "aye girrrrrrrl," he says over and over again finally he stops and says, "Fuck you bitch how you a hoe and acting stuck up?"

As she walks off I could have smacked the shit out of Stretch. I said, "What the fuck man? Why would you do that shit?"

"Mcfluzieeeeeeee," Stretch couldn't stop laughing.

"Man get the fuck out my truck and walk back."

Stretch continues to laugh while getting out the truck and walking towards the school. I got in the driver's seat closed the door and just sat there. I saw Stretch chasing after Rochelle and continue to try talking to her. I sat in my car for about an hour waiting for the game to start. I get text messages from Erica and Bam.

Text Messages

04:48pm Bam: *U a dirty nigga for not fuckin with me after school*
05:20pm Erica: *Where are you?*
05:35pm Bam: *Nigga come fuck with us after the game*
05:40pm Bam: *Meet me at the gym parking lot after the game fool*

Now that I got the rest of my night planned out I headed over to the school and went into the game. Both teams were still in the locker room. I found Erica in the stands and caked it with her until the game started.

Stretch and my other home boys got up and walked around but I couldn't. I knew that if I did Erica would wanna go and I didn't wanna run into one of my other bitches.

Halftime came around and my nigga Biggs was Homecoming King. I wanted to go down to the field but I couldn't take that chance. I stayed at the top of the bleachers with my girl until the game was over and we headed to the exits. On my way out Indo approached me, "Nigga you riding out?"

"Yea but let me finish talking to wifey." I said that hoping I would get cool points from her. Wrong.

Why did this nigga ask me right in front of my girl? She still had a fucked up attitude even after I kicked it with her the whole game. She walked away while saying, "Why don't you fuck yo boys tonight?"

I knew if I chased her down I wasn't gonna be able to get rid of her so fuck it, I let her walk. Indo and I walked to my truck got in and drove around to pick Rico, Bam, Rell, and Scoops up. When they got in the truck Scoops says, "Cuh? We gotta knock one of those valley niggas out," everyone in the car started to get crunk.

I drove to 7eleven and parked my truck across from the school. We walked down the road and posted up in front of a neighborhood sign. They lit up a blunt and smoked. I'm tossing my miniature baseball bat up in the air and catching it. "I'ma kill one of them Valley niggas wait til one walk by," said Indo.

I saw a nigga across the street with a purple and white hoodie on, Oak Valley colors. I try to distract everybody by telling them about Rochelle but it didn't work. Rell points out the dude across the street. *I'm thinking I hope this nigga runs I ain't wanna be an accessory to murder.* The dude crosses the street to our side. *What the fuck is he thinking? Does he not see a group of up to no good niggas standing here?*

"Shrimp you gonna earn your stripes today blood," said Rell.

"What that mean?"

"Either you take this nigga out or we take you out!"

We all started walking towards this dude. I put the bat behind my back. I knew I had to knock this nigga out but with this bat I was for sure to do it. As we got closer I heard Bam whisper, "If you hit him with the bat you gonna kill him nigga."

A sense of doubt took over my body, he was right. As we got right in front of the dude I couldn't do it. I walked passed him. Before I could even think to turn around and hit him, Bam walks to the side of him and knocks him out cold.

He was on the ground shaking. I see cars stopping. I could tell it was people from the game. "Hit that nigga Shrimp," said Bam. I took the bat and started delivering blows to his back and rib cage. I went crazy, I snapped. Everyone else ran but I stayed continuing to stomp and hit him with the bat. Rico grabbed me off him and we all ran through the neighborhood and to the back way to 7eleven.

79

Once we got a safe distance away everyone started bragging. "Shrimp went crazy with the bat he snapped," said Indo.

Everyone was laughing. *Was I finally in? Do I still gotta prove myself?*

Rell wasn't happy with my performance he said, "Nigga you still ain't steal off on him Cuh."

Before I could respond Bam says, "I knew that nigga and I ain't like him, I had to let him feel it."

Rico says, "Pause, No homo," and everyone started laughing.

Everyone respected and agreed with Bam but me. I knew Bam just saved me. We made it back to 7eleven and my truck was gone, Mcfluzie. I went in to ask the store clerk what happened and he said it had been towed. Everyone began to walk home in different directions and I went with Bam. *How was I gonna get my truck back? I ain't have money like that.*

"You know you don't gotta prove shit. You not built for this shit man," says Bam.

"I know you looked out for me I appreciate it."

"I knew you ain't have the heart or strength to knock that nigga out." We both laughed and joked about it till we made it to the front of my neighborhood. I went to dap him up and he was trying to do some kind of handshake. "Nigga do yo hand like this and then like this." He was teaching me the Clique handshake. "You one of us now nigga get you a red flag Cuh." He dapped me up, we did the handshake again, and he said, "Bllllllllaaaaaattt," as we parted ways.

I got home went to my room and it looked like a tornado had been through it. I looked in my dresser drawer and my condoms box was empty. I raced over to Stretch's room to open the door, it was locked. I reached in my wallet, grabbed my school ID to open the door, opened it and said, "Why you take my condoms nigga?"

"I'll get you some more tomorrow."

That wasn't a good enough answer for me. I walked over to his bed pulled the covers off and said, "You gonna get my shit now!" I realized he had a bitch in the bed with him when I pulled the covers off. I said while laughing, "Ooooohhhhhh, so you using my shit on this bitch huh?" I go cut on the lights, turn around and said, "Mcfluzie! Is that Rochelle? Stretch you a dirty nigga."

CHAPTER 9

WHAT THAT RED BE LIKE

"Having friends involved in gangs and wanting to be a part, seeking safety and/or protection from bullies, rival gangs, family members, or others and having power in numbers are some reasons teens join gangs. It's not that simple to join. There is an initiation process and trying to skip that and claim something you are not can carry severe consequences."

You couldn't tell me shit! I'm in school with my red tee, blue jeans, timbs, and red flag hanging out my back right pocket. I walked up to Rico do our handshake and said, "What up blood?" *Was I doing too much? Did I say that shit right?* From the reaction I got from Rico it seemed like I was.

With a grin on his face Rico says, "Cuh? You gonna ride out with us tonight?"

He knew I was the only way that they was gonna ride out anywhere. I paused for a second to think about it and said, "Ok, where we going?"

"We gon hit some licks."

I didn't know what hitting licks meant but to me I assumed we would be getting up with some bitches. After school I went to pick Temeaka up from her school and went back to her crib with intentions to smash. Smashing her became a ritual for me at least once a week. I would get up with her and smash being that her peoples never got home until after six.

Today out of all the days was different. We made it to her crib, went up to her bedroom and usually at this point it would be on. I lay back on her bed with just my ballin shorts and socks on and she was in the bathroom. "You better hurry up and come get this dick before your people come home."

Temeaka comes out the bathroom with the same thing she had on when she went in. After looking closely I realized that she was crying. I said, "What's wrong?" She sat down on the end of the bed with her back turned to me. I moved up and put my arm around her.

With tears now flowing down her face she says, "I don't know why you hang with Bam and them, they gonna get you killed or locked up."

Did this chick really care? What did she really have to tell me? I responded, "This ain't got anything to do with them. Who you Fucking?"

She stood up over me and started screaming for me to get out. *What was this chick's problem?* I stood up, put my clothes on, headed out the house, and to my truck. Some shit was not right. Maybe she was forcing me out the house so another nigga could come over. I drove around the corner and waited for about two hours.

I was wrong. *What the fuck was going on?* I called Temeaka's phone back to back and no answer. I texted her.

Text Messages

06:25pm Me: *Why you gotta act like that?*
06:31pm Me: *If it's another nigga just say so. Don't waste my fucking time.*

Fuck it; it was time to take my mind off the bullshit. I called Bam to see where he was at and made my way to get up with him and the crew. When I made it out Woodridge I pulled up to Scoops house where everyone was. I got out the car and began dapping everyone up first Bam, then Scoops, Rell, Indo, Chubs and Rico. I saw a couple of other niggas smoking in the cut. I gave them a head nod but they just looked at me and turned their heads. I asked Chubs, "Yo who them niggas in the cut?"

His eyes grew big, "Yo that's the OG."

I had no idea what an OG was. I asked Chubs with a confused face, "What's an OG?"

Chubs laughed and said, "Nigga that's Big Keef the OG of the hood!"

Still with my question not answered I left the topic alone. We began small talk and lit up a blunt. I looked back in the cut and noticed Big Keef and his niggas was gone. I began to open up a little more now that I knew I was around just my niggas. Rico started talking bout the bitches he had but this nigga was known to lie on his dick.

"What y'all lil niggas smokin on?"

I turned around and it was Big Keef. I was nervous as shit, he joined our conversation and started smoking with us. I knew I had to get out of there. I didn't feel comfortable and plus I wasn't from out Woodridge. I said, "Yo, y'all niggas ready to ride out? I gotta be to work in the morning."

Big Keef said, "Where y'all niggas going?"

Before I could answer Rico said, "We fin to hit some licks."

Big Keef said, "Y'all niggas be safe," then continued to dap everyone up with the set handshake. When he made it to me I go to dap him up then turned around and walked away. "Yo who you nigga? You ain't from out here." I waited a little bit to answer thinking that Bam or someone would answer the question. Nobody said a word. Big Keef walked closer to me, "So you bang nigga?"

"Yea I bang," I said not knowing what that meant.

Big Keef then walked up to me face to face and asked me, "What that red be like?"

Now I heard Chubs, Bam, and Rico ask niggas this before but I never paid attention to what the answer they got was. I could smell this nigga breath, "Nigga I said what that red be like?"

I looked over at Bam and Rico, they had looks on they face like you on your own nigga. I knew I had to respond quickly so I said, "Beautiful."

With a squinted up look on his face Big Keef said, "What the fuck did you say that red be like?"

I looked him in the eyes with confidence and said, "That red be beautiful."

His homeboys that he was with busted out laughing. Big Keef had a look on his face like he wanted to laugh but didn't. "Get this nigga the fuck from round here," said Big Keef.

Rico walked up to Big Keef whispered something in his ear and they walked off. I'm standing still about ready to shit my pants. Rico comes back laughing, "Nigga you said beautiful? Bam what the fuck you done taught this nigga?"

Everyone started laughing and made their way to my truck. After we all get in the truck I tried to change the subject. I asked Rico," Did you hit the bitches up?"

"What bitches?"

I looked around at other niggas faces who were confused like me and said, "I thought you said we was gone hit a lick?"

Everyone in the truck started laughing uncontrollably. "Nigga hit a lick mean robbing niggas fool," said Bam.

I couldn't even say nothing, I felt dumb as hell. "Hey Beautiful drive out Stone lake Plantation," said

Rico. I knew Stone lake Plantation was a rich neighborhood. *What were we about to do out there?* I didn't say anything I just proceeded to drive.

When we made it out there Rico instructs me to drive slowly. He then tells me to pull up to this brick house on the corner. I pulled up to the house parked and cut my lights out. Rico tells everyone that he was gonna go check the house out and signal everyone else in. He gets out the car, creeps up to the house, looks in the garage, and goes around the back of the house. Minutes later he comes out the garage door and waves for everyone to come in.

I took my keys out the ignition and began to get out. "What the fuck you doing Shrimp? Stay yo ass in here and be the lookout," said Bam.

They all made their way in the house. I was nervous as all hell. Ten minutes go by and still nobody came out. I saw the lights come on in the house. I started the truck up. I saw Chubs fat ass come running out the house then the rest of them followed. They all had bags full of shit. Everyone got in the truck but Rico was missing. I asked, "Where the fuck is Rico?"

I saw the garage door open and this nigga started rolling a miniature dirt bike down the driveway. They loaded it up in the back of my truck and we drove off. As we were leaving the block I saw people's house lights coming on so I started speeding out the neighborhood. "Shrimp run me to the crib," said Bam.

I could hear police sirens all around; they had to be responding to the call of us breaking in that house. We stopped by Woodridge, everyone dropped they shit off and got back in my truck to take Bam home.

We made it to Bam's crib everyone daps him up and he gets out. I drove a couple of blocks up and parked. Rico lights up a blunt and they all started smoking. "I'm bout to run up in some of these cars," said Scoops. We all got out and we started checking all the cars that were unlocked on the block and going through them. "Nigga I found some shit," said Scoops. He pulled out his pocket a .380 handgun.

We all headed back to the truck to look at it further. "Y'all niggas hot," said Rico.

Scoops passes the gun around to everyone and Chubs says, "I'm bout to go and find me one."

We all got out again and Rico says he was gonna stay behind and talk with his girl on the phone.

About five minutes into looking through cars we see blue lights around the corner. We hit the corner to look and see what happened and a police car rolls up behind us. The officer says through the intercom, "Put your fucking hands up and don't move."

The officer then proceeds to get out the car and two more cars pull up. The officer tells us to walk down to the truck and sit on the curb. Me, Scoops, Rell, Indo, Chubs, and Rico are now sitting on the curb. Five cops were standing at a distance talking while another searched my truck. The officer that was searching my truck calls the officers over to the other side of the truck. After talking for a couple of minutes they come back around and this red headed white cop named Officer Eden says, "Who's fucking gun is it?"

Nobody said a word. It remained quiet for about five minutes. Another cop says, "All you mother fuckers going to jail if we don't get to the bottom of this."

They tell us all to get up and keep our hands behind our head. Officer Eden says, "Who's truck is this?"

I replied, "It's mine."

He then told me to stand up. The other officers then split everyone up to interrogate us. Officer Eden walks up to me and says, "It's just you and me who's gun is it?"

"Im just the driver and I aint never see anyone with a gun."

"Someone will snitch, if not you will take the charge because it's your truck."

They brung everyone back together and sat us down. The officers huddle up and then one of the officers walked up to Scoops, tells him to stand up and turn around. The officer began reading him his rights, handcuffed him and put him in the police car.

Officer Eden walks up to us, throws the keys at me and says to us, "That red y'all gangbangers wear has no loyalty." The officers all started laughing while they made their way to their cars and then drove off.

We all looked at each other knowing that it could've been anyone of us that snitched. We all get back in the truck. As I drove to drop everyone off there was nothing but pure silence. We made it out Woodridge they all get out and nobody says a word to each other. I made it back home, walked in my room, threw my phone on the charger, and got ready to lay it down for the night.

I got in my bed and powered my phone on. I had a bunch of missed call alerts from Stretch and Bam. I didn't wanna be bothered with Bam because I didn't want to talk about what happened, and I definitely didn't wanna hear Stretch bitch about me hanging with The Clique. Another text message came through and it read.

Text Messages

01:15am Temeaka: *I'm sorry I acted the way I did today but I didn't know how to tell you or wat to do :(*

I'm thinking to myself this bitch done cheated on me. I hear another notification come in.

Text Messages

01:25am Temeaka: *I'm Pregnant :'(*

CHAPTER 10

GRADUATION

"Graduating from high school is a major achievement in life but what you do after that can make or break you."

"Christopher Griffin the Third," as my name was called through the speakers in the convention center I felt nervous. I wasn't nervous to be walking across the stage but to have my government name called. I had to redeem myself for those out there who would think that I was soft because my name was Christopher. As I stepped out of the line and made my way across the stage it hit me. I had to be remembered. I had to go down in history at Greenville High School as Shrimp Daddy Pimp. I saw Mr. White standing across the stage with my diploma in his hand and Super Cop Johnson standing off to the side with his hands behind his back at parade rest.

There was no way that Super Cop Johnson was gonna run on stage and tackle the shit out of me like he did when I was fighting Muhammad, and Mr. White couldn't suspend me I was done with school. I made direct eye contact with Mr. White. I remember seeing a dance that Snoop Dogg had done in his last video, and I started to do the Crip Walk across the stage. The crowd went wild. Mr. White's face began to get red as he began to walk towards me. I look at Super Cop Johnson and mocked him continuing to Crip walk with my hands behind my back while smiling at him. He gave me a look like he was gonna kill me but couldn't do anything. Mr. White made his way to me and stuck his hand out to shake it.

I dapped him up pulled him in and gave him a hug, the crowd grew even louder. "SHRIMP, SHRIMP, SHRIMP, SHRIMP, SHRIMP, SHRIMP," was all you could hear from the graduates and the people in the crowd.

Mr. White whispered in my ear, "You are gonna pay for this Christopher."

I said back to him sarcastically, "We not in your house anymore cuh."

As he handed me my diploma I continued to walk across the stage and back to my seat. I knew that I would have some explaining to do to my family especially my Mom and Dad but it was worth it. I was the talk of Greenville High School but apparently to my homies my performance wasn't taken very kindly.

After my graduation ceremony before I could even make it to see my parents Rico walked up to me and says, "I see you a crab now huh?"

Before I could even respond he walks off. As if matters couldn't get any worse my parents walked up to me and my Dad says, "Jehovah does not approve of your gang banging performance you put on, you have embarrassed your family."

I looked to my Mom for remorse but she cosigned, "Christopher you have shamed this family."

We were all supposed to go to dinner after my graduation but my parents said their goodbyes and headed back home. As much as they tried to make it seem like they really had to get back home I knew their real reason for leaving was because of the way I acted at the graduation.

Even though I haven't talked to Temeaka since the last time she was acting funny at her house and sent me a text saying she was pregnant; I wanted to break the news to my parents. They were definitely not gonna talk to me after finding out I got a girl pregnant outside of marriage but I knew it was something they needed to know.

I decided that I would give them some time to get over what happened at my graduation and I would call them and break the news. When I got back home I saw Stretch, his Mom, Dad, and Carmen in the living room. I tried to walk past them and go to my room but I was stopped short of that.

"Shrimp what in the world were you thinking," said Stretch.

Carmen, his Mom and Dad started busting out laughing. I didn't find that shit to be funny especially being that according to a couple of my text messages I know a couple of females who liked it.

I headed to my room laid on my bed and just begin to stare at the ceiling. School was over. *I finally graduated from high school, what was I gonna do now?* I put my headphones on and dozed off listening to music. I woke up and it's just about midnight. I saw my notification light flashing on my phone across the room. I had three text messages.

Text Messages

09:50pm Bam: *Nigga how u supposed to be Blood and you Crip walkin?*
09:50pm Bam: *Niggas out the hood aint like that shit one bit.*
11:19pm Temeaka: *So you think you the shit dancing across the stage and u can't even check to see if I was ok?*

My nigga Bam was trippin, and everyone in The Clique has been acting real funny after what happened with Scoops getting locked up. To this day nobody knows who told the police that Scoops took it and that alone is enough to make niggas not fuck with each other like that. I wanted to hit Temeaka up but I didn't know how to or what to say to her. I decided that I was gonna give it a try anyway so I picked up the phone and called her. I said, "What's good?"

"Nothing how have you been?"

We started a little small talk and agreed to meet up the next day. Our conversation lasted all of five minutes. I couldn't even sleep that night. I had a kid on the way, my whole life was about to change. The next morning I woke up got dressed and went to work. When I got off at 5 o'clock I headed her way. I called Temeaka when I was outside her house and she came out and got inside my truck. She looked the same to me and at this point she should be almost three months pregnant. Who was I to judge, this whole pregnancy thing was new to me.

We started talking about how her life has been these past couple of weeks. She went on to tell me that before her graduation today they were told that if anyone tried anything on the stage that they would not get their diploma. This was all because of what I did yesterday at my schools graduation. We laughed and joked about it for hours. Something was different about her today she was back to the same Temeaka that I first met. The last time we talked she was evil towards me because of this whole pregnancy thing.

I couldn't wait any longer; finally I asked her, "So how is this whole pregnancy thing going?" I said with excitement, "So you gotta be about three months pregnant now right?"

She looked at me as if she seen a ghost and said, "Well that's why I wanted to see you today and tell you face to face."

Could something be wrong with my child? This bitch was gonna probably try to put me on child support

95

because I been ignoring her acting like it wasn't mine. I remained calm and asked her, "So what's wrong?"

Tears then began to run down her face. There was complete silence between the two of us for a couple of minutes. Finally she came out and said, "I'm not pregnant."

I'm thinking to myself this scandalous bitch done fucking played me. I said, "Why the fuck would you lie to me about some shit like that?"

She looked at me with tears continuing to flow from her face and said, "I had an abortion."

There was so much anger and rage that was in my body when I heard her say that. I don't condone it, but I felt like punching her right in the face. I said, "Why the fuck you didn't consult with me?"

"My Mom made me, and plus your parents would not have accepted our child because we are not married."

This bitch did not have the right to make a decision for me. I leaned my seat back and tried to gather myself. I have never been hurt like this before. I felt like all the life was sucked right out of me. She said, "Are you ok?"

I leaned forward and said, "Does it fucking look like I am?"

I could feel something wet hit my lips. I was fucking crying. I'm too hard for this shit. I can't show any emotions to these hoes. We both sat there looking at the sky through my truck window for about an hour not

96

saying anything to each other. Finally Temeaka reaches over kisses me on my lips and says, "I hope you can forgive me Shrimp." She then gets out my truck closes the door and walks off. I sat in my truck for another thirty minutes until I heard my phone ring. It was Temeaka. She said, "I need you, Can you come here?"

She continued to say to come around to her bedroom window and come in. I got out my truck and headed to the side of the house where her window was. Right when I made it to her window to knock she opens it and I climbed through. I closed the window behind me and she heads over to her bed and gets under the covers. "Get in the bed," she says. I took my shoes off, stripped down to my balling shorts, and laid in the bed beside her. She grabs my arm and places it around her.

I heard her sniffing trying to fight back the tears all night and I tried to do the same. We stayed like that all night not saying one word to each other. I didn't know why I was crying. I was hurt that my parents felt the way they did and left, and on the other hand the abortion affected me in a way that I could never imagine. I woke up around 7am and headed back home to get ready for work. On my way to work Temeaka started texting me.

Text Messages

10:01am Temeaka: *I'm sorry I hurt you :(*
10:15am Me: *You good*
10:15am Temeaka: *What you doing today?*
10:17am Me: *Work then Chillin*
10:25am Temeaka: *Tryna chill tonight?*
10:25am Me: *Yea wat u got planned*

Text Messages

10:27am Temeaka: My home girl coming over we just Chillin
10:27am Temeaka: Bring one of your homeboys
10:35am Me: Bet what time?
10:35am Temeaka: bout 930
10:46am Temeaka: Let's get a hotel room we can go half
11:01am Me: So we go from cuddling to a hotel now? Lol
11:01am Temeaka: :)

       I wasn't about to chill with Temeaka in a hotel and have a third wheel, I had to hit up one of my niggas to ride with me. I thought about Stretch but this nigga be too thirsty, he might make an attempt to try and smash Temeaka again and fuck our whole night up. Bam always say I don't hit him up when I got the bitches so today is his lucky day. I shot Bam a text even though he and everyone was mad I disrespected the set by Crip Walking.

Text Messages

11:18am Me: Wats good I got some bitches tryna chill
11:18am Me: I got a jank for u
11:42am Bam: Word
11:48am Bam: How the bitch look
12:01pm Me: She bad as fuck I wish I got her first instead of her friend
12:01pm Bam: Word she a freak?

12:15pm Me: Hell yea my nigga
12:19pm Bam: Come scoop cuh
12:29pm Me: I'ma be there when I get off at 6 I'ma call u when I'm outside

I didn't know what Temeaka's friend looked like or if she was a freak but sometimes niggas gotta take one for the team. When I got off of work I headed over to Bam's crib and picked him up. We started talking about what happened that night with Scoops and he was telling me how it was hard to trust niggas. He said, "Remember when I told you don't be out the hood without me?"

"Yea, why you say that?"

Bam looked at me with a paranoid look on his face and said, "Well nigga now is a time where I don't even feel safe so you damn sure shouldn't. Niggas is snitching and plotting on each other."

Bam then went on to say that if some shit went down like what happened with Scoops again them niggas would place the blame on me. I couldn't see my nigga Chubs and them doing that shit to me but I went on with the conversation. We were all supposed to be cool this shit would blow over. We made it to Temeaka's house. I called her and told her to come outside. Bam said, "Damnnnn Shrimp you looked out for ya boy," as he seen Temeaka come out first. Bam gets out, walks around my truck, and gets in the back seat thinking that Temeaka was the chick I put him down with.

Once he saw that she got in the front passenger seat and gave me a kiss he looked at me and said, "Mcfluzieeeeeeeee."

99

I said, "Bam this is Temeaka and Temeaka this is Bam."

They gave each other a whatever look then Bam says, "Where is Temeaka bad friend at?"

Temeaka started laughing and told Bam that she was coming. I looked out the window and here she comes. She looked bad from a distance but that can be deceiving. As she gets closer to my truck I could see her clearly and she was definitely smashable. Now that we got the first part over I hope she a freak if not I'm just gonna tell Bam he ain't smash because his game was weak. All the pressure was now on Bam, he decides his own fate.

I looked behind me and realized that Bam and her have not said a word to each other. I asked them, "Why y'all so quiet?"

Both of them just looked at me like I was stupid then Temeaka looks back and says, "Bam this my girl April, April this is Bam."

Bam sticks his hand out and says, "Nice to meet you."

She smiles and says, "Nice to meet you too."

When we made it to the hotel I go in with Temeaka and pay for the room. I got a double bedroom, I was not gonna allow them to fuck up my night. We got back in the truck and it was still complete silence between April and Bam. Temeaka said she was hungry and wanted to get something to eat. Now was the time, I was about to put April and Bam on the spot. I said, "Bam do y'all wanna chill in the room while me and Temeaka go grab the food?" Bam had a dumb founded look on his face and began smiling. I said, "So what y'all tryna do?"

With a quick response April answered for both of them and said, "Take us to the room."

I drove around to our room and dropped them off so we could go and get some food. Temeaka said that she wanted to get some pizza so we stopped at the New York Pizza spot and ordered two large pizzas. On the way back I started to ask Temeaka about April and if she was a jump. She explained that April had a man and didn't get down like that. I told her that I told Bam she was a freak and we started laughing and taking bets all the way back to the room. Temeaka said, "I bet you your boy sitting in the corner of the room mad as hell."

We started laughing all the way to the door. I knew Bam was about to be pissed. Temeaka pulled the room key out of her pocket and slides it to open the door. When we walked in all I could say was Mcfluzie.

Bam was ass naked smashing April doggy style. "My nigga Bam," I said out loud while laughing.

April and Bam quickly got under the covers and started putting their clothes on. Once they got dressed they started eating pizza with us in complete silence. "Nigga wash y'all hands before y'all start reaching y'all hands in this box," I said.

Everyone started laughing. After we all ate we lay on the bed and watched TV for a while. I don't know what Bam was gonna do but I was tryna fuck something. I get up off the bed, walked over to the TV, and cut it off.

The room was pitch black I could barely find my way back to the bed where Temeaka was. I got under the covers with Temeaka and started kissing her and began to unbuckle her belt. I helped her pull her pants off and we both get ass naked under the sheets. I rolled over on my back, she gets on top and we started kissing. She grabs my dick and slides it in her pussy and starts riding it. At this point I don't know what April and Bam are doing but they must be getting a show. We switched positions and I get on top.

I had to let Temeaka know I owned this pussy again. She starts to yell as I'm on top stroking with her legs up in the air. I turned her over again and started hitting her doggy style. I started pulling her hair and asking her, "What's my Name?" I didn't hear her say anything so I started hitting it harder and faster and asked her again while smacking her ass, "What's my Name?"

I heard, "Bam, Bam, Bam, Bam." *I'm thinking what the fuck did this bitch say?* I stopped mid stroke and I kept hearing it, "Bam, Bam, Bam, Bam."

I wiped the sweat off my face and focused in on the noise. I see Bam looking me right in my face pointing at me from his bed while he was hitting April doggy style. She was screaming his name and he was smacking her ass. I couldn't let this man out shine me. I continued to smash Temeaka. This was no longer a battle of whose bitch could stream the loudest. This was now about who will cum first. Bam always talks shit to everyone about how he be smashing all these chicks and be going all night and he was not gonna let me prove him wrong.

We both were staring each other dead in the face as we had both our girls bent over doggy style. We kept

102

going and about ten minutes passed. I felt myself about to cum so I tried to slow down my speed. Temeaka wasn't having that and she began to throw it back faster. I pulled out right before I was about to cum and I could hear Bam laughing, "Yeaaaahhhhh nigga," he said.

I ended up slumping over and falling asleep with Temeaka in my arms. Bam and April had to of been fucking all night at least I know I heard them up until I dozed off. I woke up to the sound of a vibration noise. I looked up thinking it was my phone, I had to get to it before Temeaka, it could be one of my other hoes. I reached over to the night stand and seen that it was Temeaka's phone that was going off. Me being the nosey nigga I am, I flipped open here phone and saw she had a couple missed calls from Pooh. I checked my phone for messages and laid back down in the bed. Temeaka was woken up by the noise, "Bae, what are you doing?"

I had to ask her who Pooh was, "Somebody named Pooh keep calling you," I said.

Temeaka made a look as if she was aggregated, "That's my cousin she want me to do her hair tomorrow."

We lay in the bed cuddled for about another hour before we got up and was ready to go. While we were getting our stuff together I noticed Bam and April ain't say one word to each other. They slept on the other bed at opposite ends. Confused as to how they fucked for hours and had nothing to say I asked Bam, "Yo y'all mad at each other or something?"

Bam looked at me with a grin on his face, "I don't love these hoes its straight business."

I couldn't quite understand his way of thinking. Temeaka and I had something special, she was gonna have my child, I couldn't ever look at her that way. I turned in the room keys and we all got back in my truck. I headed to take Bam home first, then April, and last Temeaka. Before Temeaka got out the truck she gave me a big kiss and told me she loved me, I said it back and she went in the house.

I sat there in my truck for a couple of minutes dazed. *I think I found the one. This is the first girl I ever shared true emotions with.* I got home about 3pm and I went straight to sleep. I woke up the next morning around nine in the morning. I headed to the bathroom to take a piss. I pull my dick out to piss, "ahhhhhhhhhhhhhh," I dropped down to one knee. *What the fuck was wrong?* I had to piss real bad I stood up and tried to let my piss out lightly. "Fuuuuuuuuuuuuuuckkkkkkk," I screamed. My shit was burning. I had to man up; I couldn't hold my piss all day. I sucked it up and began to piss in segments screaming at the top of my lungs.

When I finished I laid on the bathroom floor in a fetal position in tears. "Boooooooooom," the bathroom door opened up and I saw Stretch standing over me. He didn't even ask me what was wrong he already knew. "Man you let one of these hoes burn you? What a dummy, get up and go to the emergency room and get some medicine."

This nigga was to clutch and calm he must have experienced this before. "They gonna stick a q-tip up yo dick fool," he said while laughing.

My dick was the one burning and it hurt so bad I ain't even started thinking about how I got it. Once the pain weakened a little I went to my room threw a shirt and shoes on and headed to the emergency room. On my way out the house I could hear Stretch singing and laughing, "He's on Fireeee, He's on Fire, Fire, Fireeeeeeee." That shit angered me. I was thinking of the last two bitches I fucked Erica and Temeaka. If I was a betting man it was Erica.

As I was driving I called her, "Hello Stranger," she says.

"Bitch you burnt me," I said in rage.

Erica then went off like I never seen before. It couldn't have been her she was too hostile. Before I could apologize and get back in good graces she hung up. *I'm thinking to myself that this bitch Temeaka all along has been playing me like a PS2. Her friend April was a hoe so she had to be a hoe. Why was she hanging with that bitch April?* I then started to play the devil's advocate second guessing myself. *It can't be Temeaka we are in love, she was about to have my kid.*

I had to at least confront her. I called her phone no answer. Then again no answer. Finally on the third call I got an answer. "Hello," the voice I heard was deep as hell.

I paused for a minute then asked, "Who dis?"

The deep voice responded, "This is Pooh."

I remember Temeaka saying her cousin Pooh was blowing her phone up to get her hair done. Her cousin Pooh had to be a big girl her voice was too deep. I chuckled, "Pooh put my girl on the phone."

Pooh got quiet I was assuming she was handing her the phone, "Nigga, Temeaka is my girl don't call her phone again or we gone have some problems."

"Say what Cuh?" The phone was quiet, "Beep," he hung up the phone, Mcfluzieeeeee.

CHAPTER 11

CRIME DONT PAY

"If you do the crime you are expected to do the time.
Snitching is not an option."

I couldn't believe what had happened. The one girl I truly cared about and reviled my emotions to was just like the rest of these hoes. I always wondered why Bam was so cold hearted when it came to females and now I see. All I got is my niggas, they been there for me when nobody else was even my own Mom and Dad. I decided to hop in my truck and roll out Woodridge.

When I made it out there I see Bam, Biggs, and four other niggas I have seen before but didn't really know them. When I got out the truck I dapped everyone up and they introduced themselves. Their names were Thomas, Squirrel, Meech, and Snacks. As I dapped them up and heard them say their names I realized these niggas names made noise out the hood they went hard. After meeting everyone Biggs asked, "Where the hoes at cuhhhhh?"

I didn't know why this nigga was asking me this he was the star athlete. I said, "I don't got the hoes."

Before I could say anything else everyone started laughing and Snacks said, "You a lying bitch, Bam told us y'all ran train on them hoes the other night."

I was shocked. This nigga Bam can't hold water; I thought I could trust this nigga to keep quiet. I paused for a minute and said, "I'ma hit them up and see what's good for tonight."

Thomas began rolling a blunt up and we walked to the cut to smoke. As Thomas was rolling up the blunt he started talking about how he wanted to hit a couple of licks that night to get some money for the new Jordan's that was about to come out.

I saw this as a way in. If I put in work with these niggas everyone would know my name in the streets. I said, "I got the whip what's good?"

Everyone looked at me. Squirrel said, "Bet let me go get my shit I'll be back."

After finishing the blunt Thomas, Meech, Snacks, and Biggs all went in the house to change. I sat on the Green box in the cut with Bam waiting for them to get back. I was quiet for a couple of minutes then Bam says, "You are a dumb nigga. This ain't Chubs and those niggas these niggas here are straight killas."

I looked at Bam with a confused face, "We just chillin," I said.

Bam looked at me with a serious face and said, "These niggas don't chill. Don't say I didn't warn you."

When they all got back we got into my truck and rode out. I said, "Where we going cuh?"

"Let's go out Oak Valley Cuh," said Meech.

Shit was about to get real, if these niggas see an Oak Valley nigga it's a fight on sight. When we made it out Oak Valley Thomas tells me to pull up to the park and turn my lights out. I was on full alert. Everyone else was in the truck smoking, listening to music, and laughing.

I saw a guy in a black hoodie walk up to the park talking on his cellphone. "Aye Nigga turn the music down," said Snacks. He was on the phone talking with someone. After a couple of minutes Snacks gets off the phone. The guy that was at the park started walking over to my truck.

I said, "Yo, dis nigga walking up on us."

"They started laughing and Biggs said, "Chill we bout to buy some trees."

This shit didn't make sense. Why would a nigga that sells trees buy from another nigga that sells trees if he already got a lot of it? I didn't pay that shit no mind. When the guy made his way to my truck Snacks and Meech got out. I could see them on the side of the truck

109

making a transaction. After they were done the guy in the hoodie turned to walk off.

Before he could take one step Meech ran up beside him and punched him in the face. Meech and Snacks began stomping him and Squirrel opened my truck door. Meech and Snacks threw him in my truck and Biggs yelled, "Drive nigga." I hit the lights started up the truck and headed out the neighborhood.

"Drive to Oak Pond," said Meech.

As I'm driving all I could hear was screaming, I was too scared to look back. When we made it to Oak Pond which was a pond that had woods surrounding it everyone got out the truck and headed to the tree line.

Bam walks around to my side of the truck and says, "This what you started, stay here and keep the truck running."

I saw them all disappear into the tree line. I waited for about ten minutes then, "Boom, Boom, Boom." I heard three gunshots. I sat up in my seat. Running out of the tree line I see Bam, Thomas, Squirrel, Biggs, Meech, and Snacks. They get in the truck and I drive off. I didn't ask or didn't want to know what just happened, all I know is that the guy they went in with didn't come out with them.

Everyone was quiet until Biggs and Bam asked me to take them home. I was hoping these other niggas wanted to go home but to them the night had just begun. After dropping Biggs and Bam off we went driving around. They wanted to go to a nearby park to smoke so I pulled into the closest neighborhood and parked. Right when I cut the lights out a Chinese food delivery man drives pass us. He circles around the court then comes back beside my truck and parks. He sits in the car and is getting the order ready to deliver.

Thomas, Squirrel, Meech and Snacks hop out the truck. They post up on the curb like they lived out there. When the Chinese man got out to walk up to the apartments, Thomas waves him down. I could hear Thomas say it was his food and began pulling money out. Right when Thomas went to give him the money Snacks punches the Chinese man in the face and he falls. Squirrel starts running his pockets and Meech starts searching his car. I started my truck up ready to take off. "Turn over nigga," said Thomas. I don't think the Chinese man understood him. Thomas pulls a gun out and says, "Turn the fuck over bitch."

I was clinging on to my seat. *What have I got myself into?* The Chinese man was screaming and still didn't turn over, "Boom." Thomas shot him and everyone jumped into the truck. "Get us the fuck out of here," said Snacks.

I slammed my foot on the gas and sped off. Once we made it out the neighborhood they started laughing. "You shot that nigga in the ass," said Snacks.

I didn't find this shit funny we could go to jail for a long time for the shit that just happened. I couldn't show weak emotions, I pulled up to 7eleven to get some gas. When I went inside I called the only nigga who could help me which was Bam. When he answered I said, "I'm bout to come get you man, these niggas doing reckless shit I need your help."

"Nigga I told you what was gonna happen, you didn't listen now you on your own."

Before I could explain he hung up. I tried calling back several times no answer. I tried to chirp him no answer. I put $10 in my tank and went outside to fill up. When I got in the truck Snacks and Meeks was on the phone with some chicks and they wanted to go get up with them. Once they set it up they got off the phone and I turned the music up. I headed out of the 7eleven parking lot and made a right headed to the chicks house. I saw something light up behind me. I thought it was someone trying to pass so I switched lanes.

I see the lights again and this time they were police lights flashing so I pulled over. "Everybody shut the fuck up and stay calm," said Snacks.

The officer sat in his car for a couple of minutes and then walked up to my truck. This nigga looked familiar it was the same red head cop Officer Eden from the night Scoops got locked up. He leant into the driver seat, flashed the flashlight on everybody's face, and told me to step out the truck. When I got out he looked at me and said, "You hanging with the real criminals tonight," and laughed.

He instructed me to get back in the truck, walked to his car, and called for backup. Everyone in the truck was quiet but I could tell they all been here before. As the other police cars come they all huddled up and then proceeded to the truck. Officer Eden then asked if he could search my truck. Before I could say anything Meech said, "Fuck no."

Officer Eden replied, "I smell weed everyone get the fuck out the truck one by one."

As we got out the officers cuffed us one by one and sat us on the curb. Three officers then begin to search my truck. This was like De Ja Vu. The officers came out the truck smiling and walked up to us. One of the officers says, "You guys are fucked. The truck has three firearms and lots of weed."

Officer Eden signals for the cops to load us up in the cars. As they take us Snacks screams out, "Don't say a fucking word."

Officer Eden grabs me and says, "You riding with me blood," with a smirk.

He puts me in the back seat and turns the heat on to the max. I could barely breath it was so hot. I started kicking the door and screaming, it felt like I was dying. I'm sure everyone else was experiencing the same shit. These cops were dirty as fuck.

I sat up and I could see them huddled up talking. All the officers made their way back to their cars. Officer Eden gets in and I say, "What the fuck you tryna kill me? I can't breathe."

Officer Eden cuts the heat off, turns around, and says, "Christopher, I know you are at the wrong place at the wrong time hanging with the wrong hoodlums. If you don't snitch and bring these guys down you will be going away to jail for a very long time."

"I ain't do shit; those guns and weed ain't mines."

He looked at me with a serious face and said, "There has been two shootings tonight, both victims are in critical condition, that's attempted murder, and if they

113

die it's a murder charge. Become a witness or become a defendant."

The whole ride to the police station Officer Eden didn't say one word. When we arrived he took me into the police station and into the interrogation room. He put both hands down on the table looked me in my face said, "You know what to do," and walked out the room. After that door closed behind him I saw my life flash before my eyes. *Should I Snitch and walk free or live by the street code and don't say shit?*

CHAPTER 12

I DIDNT SNITCH

"Once you are labeled a snitch you can never shake that reputation."

Waking up in the morning felt unreal. I thought everything that happened was a dream. I tried lying back down and couldn't fall asleep. I was facing reality. Those guys that got shot last night could be dead and I'm labeled a snitch. I had to go pick my truck up and head out Woodridge to clear my name. There was only one problem; I had to make up a lie to Stretch as to why my truck got towed.

Stretch was the only person who could take me. I headed over to Stretch's room and was direct with him, "My truck got towed for not parking in visitor parking last night, can you take me to get it?"

"Nigga, the police dropped you off last night, I ain't stupid nigga."

I went on to explain to Stretch that I waved down the officer for a ride home because I had no way to get home. From the expression on his face I knew that he didn't believe me but he also didn't feel like arguing. Stretch agreed to take me, I got dressed and we got in his car. The whole car ride he was on the phone talking to some chick whispering sweet nothings in her ear. This nigga used the same game on every chick he talked to but for some reason he was still pulling them.

When we got to the tow yard I reached to dap Stretch up. Stretch tells the person on the phone to hold on. He looks at me and says, "I heard some shit went down last night and everybody saying you snitched. Lay low those niggas are dangerous."

I smiled and said, "Ok, I'm good."

After dropping $225 to get my car out my pockets were hurt. I was supposed to go to work but I'ma have to call in, I had to head out the hood to straighten shit out. When I made it out Woodridge I see the crew chillin at the basketball court. It was Chubs, Rico, Rell, Indo, and Bam. I got out the truck and walked up to them to dap them up. I thought niggas would be acting funny but everything looked cool.

We stood on the side of the court talking about what happened the day before and niggas was giving me mad props. Rell said, "Shrimp be putting in that work."

I was the talk of the hood. It was one nigga that didn't show me any love and that was Bam. It caught me by surprise that of all people it was Bam hatin. Everybody was talking about the Clique party some nigga named Hammer was throwing. They asked me if I was going and I told them they needed to give me gas money.

Everybody agreed to give me $5 so I agreed to go. They went and got changed while I sat in the truck with Bam and Rico. Bam said, "You know these niggas know you snitched right?"

I looked at Bam and said, "Stop hating nigga. We were putting in work last night while yo ass went in the house scared."

Bam looked at me like he was about to punch me in the face and said, "Don't say I ain't tell you."

"Rico started laughing and said, "Shrimp I would listen to yo boy before it's too late."

I wasn't tryna hear that shit. If I was a snitch then niggas would of tried to get me already, niggas was showing me mad love out the hood. Chubs, Rico, Rell, and Indo returned back to the truck. Indo asked me can I go pick his cousin Mike up so he can go to the party with us.

"He got gas money?"

"Yea and if he don't I got you."

We headed to Mike's house with the music blasting loud, we was getting live in the truck. Rell was talking about how many bitches was gonna be at the party and how live it was last year. When we made it to Mike's house he was sitting outside with a wife beater on. Mike walked up to my window dapped me up and said, "I heard about you nigga." I didn't know how to take that. When he got in he asked me could I take him to the mall to get a shirt. He told me he would give me some money on the Pedro. I was cool with that; it meant more money in my pocket.

We made it to the mall and Mike told me to park in the rooftop parking so we could be in and out. After we parked we all went in to the mall and into this store called, "Throwbacks." We all sat outside of the store on the bench while Mike was on the phone and looking for a shirt. The mall was filled with bad bitches and it seemed like everybody we knew that was walking by us was going to Hammer's party. When Mike came out he told the person on the phone, "I'm coming now just have that shit ready," and then he hung up the phone.

We headed up the escalator and then outside to the parking lot. As we made it into the parking area I saw two niggas walking towards us say, "Bllllllllaaaaattttttt."

Mike yelled back at them, "What's poppin my niggas?"

Everybody walked up to them to dapp them up and I did the same. After we dapped each other up Mike walks a few feet away with the two guys and starts whispering. Bam walks closer to them and over hears what they are saying and says in a loud angry voice, "That shit ain't going down."

Bam begins arguing with Mike and the two guys. Rico walks up and tells everyone to calm down. One of the guy's pull a gun out, drops it to his side and says, "Fuck that shit, niggas snitching on my cousin they got to get it."

Mike puts his arm around the two guys and walks off with them. We all get back into my truck. Nobody was saying shit; everyone had strange looks on their faces. Mike walks up, gets in the truck, and I started the truck up. "Shrimp go home nigga we will find another way to the party," said Bam.

Before I could say anything Mike says, "What for? Niggas ain't gonna touch you, they my peoples you good with me."

Mike did just defuse this situation that just happened. I believed him. I begin to head to the party. "Don't come running to me when shit happen," said Bam.

Mike looked at me and says quietly, "You good with me nigga."

Mike directed me on how to get to the party. When we got there it was packed. We all get in line Rico, Mike, Rell, Bam, Indo, and Chubs all pay to get in. I walked to the door payed the security $10 he pats me down and I walked through. The hoes were in the party throwing it. We all walked around the party looking for chicks to dance with. We found a spot on the wall and we all posted up.

Across the party I could see two dudes that looked like Meech and Squirrel. I had to go talk to them.

119

I got off the wall and headed over there. As I got closer I realized it was them. When they noticed me Squirrel whispered something in Meech's ear and then walked off. I walked up to Meech and extended my hand to dap him up. I said, "What's good Meech?"

He didn't even raise his hand. He looked me right in my face and said, "Get the fuck out my face, Snitch!"

I didn't know what else to say but, "I didn't snitch."

Meech completely ignored me so I turned around and walked off. I had to find Bam and tell him what just happened. I saw Bam in the corner getting a dance. I rushed up to him and said, "Yo Meech told me to get out his face because he thinks I snitched."

Bam moved the girl out the way quick and told me to leave now. I saw Bam walk quickly up to Meech and started whispering in his ear. Maybe Bam could straighten things out. When I turned around to walk over to where the rest of the crew was it felt like someone hit me with a block of concrete. I fell down to the ground and saw the whole crowd close in on me. I felt a chair hit me and I could see nothing but unfamiliar people punching and kicking me. I balled up on the floor and the kicking and punching got worse. I felt somebody grab, and pick me up in the air. This guy was about to slam me. I could feel myself moving through the crowd and the next thing I know I was outside.

This big muscular nigga sat me down on the ground, it was Biggs. He looked at me with a serious face and said, "Go home these niggas will kill you."

Biggs turned around and went back into the party. I got up pissed. *Who was this nigga that sucker punched me? This nigga needed to see me one on one.* I waited till the security wasn't paying attention and snuck back in the party behind them. The first person I seen was Mike. I walked up to him and said, "Find the nigga that snuck me. Tell him I wanna see him one on one."

I was walking through the party mugging everyone. Mike came up to me with this nigga named Louis. Louis looked at me and said, "I knocked yo snitching ass out nigga, see me."

The crowd began to close in on us. I squared up with him. The crowd ends up pushing us outside to the parking lot. I square back up with Louis again and out of nowhere someone punched me in the jaw. Meech said, "Yea nigga you wanna snitch on my cousin?"

People in the crowd started saying, "Oh this the nigga that snitched? Get the heat nigga."

People were running to their cars to get their guns. Other niggas were tryna rush me and get a hit in. Mike put his arm around me and told everyone, "Ain't nobody touching this nigga he gon fight Louis one on one."

Bam walked up to me and said, "Don't fight this nigga here niggas gone bank yo ass."

I yelled out loud to Louis, "Meet me out Woodridge nigga."

Mike escorted me to my truck and everyone that rode with me got in after. As we were leaving the parking lot I saw 5-6 niggas with guns in their hands. They wanted to shoot but didn't only because of who else was in the truck. We hit the highway and headed back to Woodridge. Squirrel, Meech, and Louis were driving beside us. I kept looking at them as if I wanted to kill them. As we got close to Woodridge Mike was hyping me up. "Shrimp you better fuck that nigga Louis up he a bitch."

Bam grew angry and said, "Shrimp, go the fuck home man. Why would you go out another nigga hood and fight him?"

Mike said, "Nigga if anybody jumps in I'ma beat they ass it's a straight one on one."

Rico said, "Foreal these niggas gonna beat yo ass Shrimp. I ain't even gon lie."

I ignored all that shit Rico and Bam was talking. I had to get this nigga Louis. We pulled up in Woodridge. Meech and those niggas trailed us. "Shrimp if you fight this nigga you on ya own. I warned yo dumb ass. I ain't helping you I'ma let them beat yo ass," said Bam.

We pulled up in the first court of the neighborhood and got out. It was already like fifteen people outside but I paid that shit no mind. Louis and Squirrel got out their car and Meech stayed in the back seat watching. I walked up to Louis and squared up with him. "I'ma kill yo snitch ass," said Louis.

I swung my right hand and caught him in the face. He swings back with his right and catches me. We started going blow for blow and I was getting the best of him. I started getting tired so I charged in to scoop him. I lifted his feet off the ground and dumped him on his back. He rolled over on top of me and hit me two times in the face. I started swinging back with my back on the ground. He grabbed both my hands and pinned them on the ground.

I felt someone kick me in my side I looked up and it was Squirrel. I yelled out, "One on One."

Squirrel said, "Fuck that shit you fucking snitch."

I tried pushing Louis off of me. I was looking around me and saw Bam, Chubs and the crew just standing there watching. I looked the other way and saw Mike. He started running towards me cocked his foot back and kicked me in the face. I blacked out. All I remembered was I heard him say, "Snitch," right before he kicked me. When I came to I could feel people stomping and hitting me. I saw Chubs, Indo, Rell, Mike, Louis, Squirrel, and a couple of other niggas I couldn't recognize all attacking me. While I was still getting hit I tried standing up and swinging back.

I made it to my feet, Indo catches me in my jaw and I fell back down. I tried getting back up again but my body was too weak. I looked up and I could see Meech creeping up slowly with a gun in his hand. "The police coming," someone yelled.

Everyone scattered, I laid down on my stomach with my vision blurred. I yelled out, "Baaaaaaam." I looked up and he was standing right in front of me. I said, "Can you drive me home?"

Bam looked at me with a remorseful look and said, "The police coming I told yo ass man. I fucking told you." Bam then ran off behind everyone else.

The police came and stood over top of me. "We already know who did this to you all you have to do is say their names," said one cop.

Another cop stood over top of me it was Officer Eden. He said, "Son do you need to go to the hospital?"

"No, I'm fine officer."

I began to try and get up, he put my arm around his neck, another officer did the same with my other arm, and they helped me to my truck. They opened my truck door and sat me down. Officer Eden says, "Now let's start with Meech, who else did this to you?"

"I don't know who did it. I was just walking through the neighborhood and some guys ran up on me."

Officer Eden smacked my truck door leaned in and said, "These guys just tried to kill you. We can put those niggers away for this shit like the other two little niggers Thomas and Snacks." I leaned my head back on my seat, shrugged my shoulders like I didn't know anything, and closed my eyes. "So be it, next time we won't respond, I'll just let y'all niggers kill each other," said Officer Eden.

The officers went and huddled up for a couple of minutes talking then they got in their cars and drove off. I could barely even move but I knew I had to make it home. *They could come back and get me again.* I started the truck up and headed home. When I made it in the driveway I called Stretch. He said, "What's good Shrimp?"

I was in so much pain all I could say was, "HELP."

124

Stretch said, "What's wrong?"

I responded back in a faded voice, "I'm outside."

I leaned back in my seat and I could hear the house front door swing open as Stretch came running out. When Stretch made it to me he said, "Ohhhhhh Shit Shrimp what did they do?"

I could see tears coming down his face but I was too weak to respond. Stretch pulled me out my truck, placed my arm around his neck, and guided me into the house. As soon as we made it into the living room I dropped to the ground. "Maaaaaaaaaaaaaa, Daaaaaaaaaaad, Shrimp is dying," said Stretch.

The tears continued to flow from Stretch's face. His Mom and Dad came running in the living room. "Ohhhhh myyyyy godddddddddd Shrimp," Stretch's Mom began crying and yelling. Stretch's dad grabbed me, picked me up, and took me outside to his car. He laid me in the backseat and began taking me to the hospital. I couldn't remember anything after that. When I woke up I had a cast on my right arm, a bandage wrap around my head, and I was plugged up to all kinds of machines.

I opened my eyes with my blurred vision and all I could see was a guy my age standing there, "I didn't snitch," I said.

It was Stretch, he walked up closer to me and now I could see him clearly. He said, "I told you not to hang with these dudes but you know I'm always gonna be here for you bro."

I could hear Stretch's Dad and Mom conversation about something that had happened on the news. The room grew quiet and I could hear the reporter say that there were two shootings over the weekend that led to one dead and another in critical condition. They had two suspects in custody with four more that the police are looking for. The reporter said the names of the two in custody were Hakiem Anderson, and Lamont Moore. My heart stopped. Stretch turned to look at me and words could not even explain the look he gave me. Stretch walked towards me slowly and said real low, "That's Thomas and Snacks!"

CHAPTER 13
LOST CAUSE

"A lot of teens go thru a time in life where they are trying to find themselves. Despite all the advice given some things people just have to learn on their own."

After the events that took place between me and the Clique it really freighted Stretch's family. They thought it was best for me to move out and in with my parents in Owens Mills, Maryland. I needed some me time. I needed to discover who I am and what I wanted to be in life. After staying with my parents for about six months, I got accepted into the Baltimore County Fire Department. It was a real hard process but it made me into a man. All that foolish stuff was behind me. Even though my life still wasn't in line to the standards of Jehovah I have made a complete change. This is probably the main reason why I am where I am today.

My parents didn't approve of the way I was living which in a sense kept me distant from them. After about a year I ended up moving out. I had one thing I couldn't control and that was the thirst for these hoes. While I was living with my parents in Owens Mills I met this bad chick named Lashawn. She was studying to become a witness like myself but like me she lusted for sex. The first time I ever had sex with here she got pregnant. I don't regret it one bit but I know I am not ready to become a father. I use to bag chicks off of Myspace back in VA but Baltimore was a nesting ground.

What made matters bad for me was the fact that I had my own crib with my roommate Jeff. Jeff was a cool calm and collected dude that was mad laid back. He worked at Lowe's and did his R&B music on the side. With every person there is baggage and that was his cousin Blow. Blow was a young dumb and immature nigga. Now my past was the same, I was only two years older than him but this nigga was hot.

I saw a little me in him so I took him under my wing to try to guide him so he wouldn't go thru what I did. The hard thing about tryna give someone like him advice is that even at his young age he has already seen and done it all. VA goes hard no doubt but the streets of Baltimore are just about as real as it gets.

Between me going to work and trying to pursue a career as a firefighter I had a roster of bitches. My main chicks at this time was a chick named Phoenix and another chick that I met that just got out of jail named Crystal aka Blood Homie. Blood Homie was brown skinned with long box braids, had a tomboyish look like Aaliyah, was a stone cold freak, and could be very intimidating.

128

Phoenix was this young caramel skin complexion 18 year old chick still in high school, and not to mention she was my baby moms Lashawn best friend. Phoenix's prom was coming up and I agreed to take her to it. I was gonna make this the best night of her life. When I arrived at her house on prom day it was filled with her mom, dad, aunts, cousins, brothers, sisters, and friends. It felt awkward for me not because I was older than her, but because everyone knew she had a man, and that I got Lashawn pregnant. I had gotten her best friend pregnant but as always my intentions were just to smash, and it felt like everyone knew.

Phoenix looked beautiful. I seen her before in regular clothes and she couldn't dress or keep up with her hair to save her life. Now she looked like a damn supermodel after all the makeup and shit. We say our goodbyes and head to her school prom. I had to set the tone quick, she had to know it was about to go down. "Phoenix," I said.

She looked with a smile and said, "Wats up?"

I paused for a second, "How long did it take you to get that dress and all that makeup on?"

"Hours."

I looked at her with a smirk, "Well how long will it take you to come up out of all that?"

It was quiet as all hell in the car. I stared at her for an answer until finally she says, "How fast can you take it off?"

I wanted to hit a u turn and head to my crib immediately but I didn't want to ruin her prom moment. We went back and forth exchanging sexual taunts all the way until we arrived at her prom. Once we made our entrance I slow danced with her for two songs and then I sat down and drank punch while she partied with her classmates. My main mission was to avoid my baby mom's but that didn't last long.

I was mad when I seen her not because she had a dude all over her but because she was pregnant, and this thirsty nigga she was with was definitely gonna smash on prom night. I sucked it up because I knew the same thought was going thru her head. Her once best friend was about to smash the homie. About one hour in Phoenix walks up to me reaches her hand out as if she wanted a dance and said, "Let's go I'm ready for some us time." We made our way to the exit all while she was saying her goodbyes to her friends, and boy did she have some bad friends.

We hopped in my truck and made our way back to my crib. She had no idea what she was about to experience. I told Jeff and Blow to have the living room and shit clear. A lot of hoes hated that walk of shame. They knew that everyone in the house was aware of what is about to go down and sometimes they wanna be under the radar. We made our way to my apartment door kissing and feeling all over each other. I stick my key in the door and opened it all while still kissing her. I could hear the TV on in the living room but paid it no mind.

All of a sudden she stops. I look at her and I could see her staring behind me. I turned around and saw this nigga Blow on the couch with just his boxer briefs on and no shirt eating a box of chocolates that I had bought for tonight. Blow started laughing and said, "What y'all niggas just got married?"

I looked at him with a state of shock and said, "Mcfluzie."

I was about to go off on him but Blow is not the type nigga you wanna embarrass, he will blow ya spot up and expose all your business. I looked at him and sarcastically said, "Them chocolates look good as hell."

He sat up like he was about to talk shit, but before he could I directed Phoenix to my room. As we approached my door I put my hand over her eyes and with my other hand opened the door. Now anybody that knows me knows I'ma have the rose pedals, the chocolates, and the ice. I had to step my game up. When I removed my hand she was shocked.

I had the roses sprinkled all over, with chocolate minus what Blow took, ice, but what was the deal closer was the canopy I had over the bed. I started taking my clothes off and headed over to my bed. I crawled thru the canopy and lay down on the bed. She quickly took off her dress and stripped down to nothing but her thong.

She came and lay beside me on the bed. I lit the candles and began to kiss her starting from her knees until I made my way to her thong. I bit her thong with my mouth and slid it off. I went straight for the box; she was wet as all hell. As I'm eating her out she begins to make loud moans while squeezing my head. I come up after about ten minutes, slide my dick in her pussy, and then begin stroking. I grabbed her legs and put them in the air, she tries to push my body away but I kept stroking harder and faster.

131

Her body started shaking all while she was trying to push my body away. She screams out, "Oh my god I'm bout to cum again."

I could feel myself about to do the same and pulled out. I came on her stomach a rolled over to the side of her. She was still moaning balled up in the fetal position. I put in that work. I ate the box for ten minutes and smashed for five. It may not seem like a long time but it was enough to get the job done on a lot of females.

After Phoenix came out of the comma I put her in she went to the bathroom to freshen up then came out and started getting dressed. I asked her why she was getting dressed and she said she had to get home before midnight. I jumped up threw some balling shorts on and we headed to my truck to take her home. It was quiet all the way until we got to her house. When I parked she looked at me as if she was mad about something. I said, "What's wrong?"

She started going off saying how she was not a hoe, I shouldn't have ran up in her raw, and if she wasn't taking birth control I could have gotten her pregnant. *My first response was to call this hoe ass bitch every name in the book and tell her to get the fuck out my car but I realized I just won the championship. I just smashed, why would I argue with this bitch?*

When she finished her rant I looked at her and said, "You looked beautiful tonight," very sarcastically.

She opened the car door, got out slammed it, stuck her head thru the window, and said very low so nobody could hear, "You fucking asshole."

I wasn't about to let this bipolar bitch fuck my night up. On my way back home I started texting Blood Homie.

Text Messages

11:50pm Me: *what's good crystal you tryna chill?*

11:51pm Blood Homie: *we can*

11:53pm Me: Where u at

11:53pm Blood Homie: *I'm at my peoples house you gonna scoop me up?*

11:55pm Me: *Address?*

12:03am Blood Homie: *1286 Martin Addams Blvd #6*

I started heading towards her peoples crib. When I got there I saw a bunch of niggas wearing red and smoking outside. I texted her.

Text Messages

12:45am Me: *I'm outside*

12:56am Me: *hurry up I ain't got all day*

1:05am Me: *you flexxin*

After texting and calling this bitch multiple times and no answer I headed to the apartment. One of the dudes that was posted outside said, "What up blood?"

I gave him a head nod and kept moving. I learned my lesson on that a long time ago. I go up to the door and started knocking and no answer. I waited about

133

two minutes and started knocking again. Somebody looked me dead in my eyes thru the blinds. I lifted my hands up. I seen Blood Homie lift the blinds up and signal me to leave. I shook my head no and signaled for her to call me. She started nodding her head yes and closed the blinds. I went around to the back of the apartment and noticed there were some broken blinds in the back window.

I walked up to the blinds and looked thru them. I could see this bitch Blood Homie cuddled up with some nigga smoking weed. My first reaction was to bust the fucking window out or run up in the crib. I remembered I was in Baltimore. I walked back to my truck and began blowing her phone up with calls and still no answer so I texted her.

Text Messages

1:23am Me: You a dirty bitch u in there laying with another nigga

Text Messages

1:23am Me: *You a Fucking J O*

1:24am Me: *yo ass making me waste gas on yo hoe ass*

I decided to turn this shit into a stakeout. I'ma find out who this nigga is. I ain't waste my time driving out here. I received a text from her about ten minutes later.

1:34am Blood Homie: *that's my peoples dumb ass. I can't chill. We going thru some family issues*

134

Text Messages

1:35am Me: *Why you wasting my time?*

1:41am Blood Homie: *Sorry I'll make it up to u*

Fuck that, I wasn't tryna hear that shit. I noticed niggas going in and out the crib and they weren't knocking either. This was my time. I walked up to the apartment and posted up in the hallway. I waited about two minutes and I walked right in. When I entered the house it was filled with smoke. I saw two niggas and three hoes on the couch smoking and watching TV. I said to them, "I got some loud for Crystal, is she here?"

These niggas was so high all they prolly heard was Crystal. One of the niggas said, "She in the back brah."

I made my way to the back and to the room I saw them in earlier. I'm outside the door and I can hear her laughing. I quickly opened the door and made direct eye contact with her. She was lying under the covers with some bum looking ass nigga. I pulled the covers off and said, "You fucking hoe bitch. So this is what you doing? Fucking with these bum ass niggas?"

The nigga got up and said, "Who you calling a bum partna?"

It was on. I needed an escape plan. Blood Homie started hugging the dude and tried calming him down. I had to make my move. I grabbed the bottom of the bed they was on and flipped it over while they were on it. I saw a small night stand beside it so I grabbed that and threw it on top of them as well. I dashed out the room closed the door, and started walking thru the living room

135

where everyone was not tryna cause a scene. "Ight fam," I said to them on the way out. They gave me a head nod and I closed the door. As soon as the door was closed I took off full speed to my truck.

The adrenaline rush had me dropping my keys. This may sound like some shit in them scary movies but when your life is on the line this shit real. Finally, I got myself together and got my truck started. I saw the nigga open the door and start running after me as I drove off. Blood Homie started calling my phone off the hook, there was no way I was gonna answer. I made it back home and laid down on my bed. I had to be to work in about four hours I had to get some sleep. I started reading all the text messages I got from Blood Homie.

Text Messages

2:15am Blood Homie: *you dead Shrimp*

2:19am Blood Homie: *we coming to see u now*

2:22am Blood Homie: *I'm sorry for hurting you*

2:30am Blood Homie: *please* answer

I wasn't worried about the threats. I didn't think she would bring someone to my house. After going thru all the messages I noticed I also had missed calls and text messages from Phoenix. After reading these messages there was no way I was going to sleep.

Text Messages

2:17am Phoenix: *I tried calling you*

Text Messages

2:21am Phoenix: *I'm sorry for how I acted but I have something to tell you*

2:23am Phoenix: *There can no longer be us I'm tryna work it out with my boyfriend*

2:25am Phoenix: *You might wanna get tested I have Syphilis.*

CHAPTER 14
TALKIN IN CODES

"They say men are dogs, but a wise man once told me, You can see a dog pee but you won't see a cat pee."

After going to get tested at the clinic for STDs all tests came back negative. Waiting for those test results took seven days and boy was they the longest seven days I ever experienced. I couldn't watch any TV, those wrap it up and get tested commercials made it so bad for me. I called out all week at work and today was my first day back. I told them I was sick. I arrived at work and like always I was late. Every time I had to deal with hearing it from one of my pillow talking ass coworkers especially from a guy named James. "Aye good to see you finally made it in," said James.

This white dude was an asshole motherfucker that got no ass but always was worried about what I had going on. When I first started at this Fire Department they use to break me down with that sarcasm. Being I was the only black guy in the department I took that shit to heart. But now that shit paid me no mind. I knew he didn't get any ass so while we use to sit around and wait for calls I use to call up bitches and talk about how I was gonna put down the murder game on em.

This shit infuriated James. In a way I was giving this nigga more ammunition to snitch and try to get me fired. Today I decided I was gonna call my bitch Keisha. Now this bitch Keisha was a single black independent chick that had a good paralegal job. The only thing wrong with this picture was her High School sweetheart. This nigga was a Class A sucka for love and would do anything for her. From time to time they would break up and Keisha would fall right into my lap. I started texting her.

Test Messages

2:03pm Me: *What's good Ma?*

2:07pm Keisha: *Nothing just chilin at work*

2:11pm Me: *How was the crime scenes today?*

With most of my bitches I had a code word I used for smashing and with Keisha it was crime scenes. We use this because she always said I put the murder game down on her pussy and with her job she dealt with murder cases a lot. My name was saved in her phone as Derrick, one of her coworkers.

139

Test Messages

2:25pm Keisha: *It was a Double Homicide out Baltimore today shit crazy.*

2:28pm Me: *Cold world tell the Boss I'm headed to lunch.*

2:31pm Keisha: *Ok will do.*

A double homicide in our code meant her dude worked both jobs today. Keisha was a master at creeping. When it was time for me to get off of work I hit the time clock and headed towards my truck. I saw James standing at his car talking to two of my other coworkers and I said, "Let me know how your night of playing video games home alone goes." James couldn't say anything back. I hit him where it hurts with that sarcasm. Nobody else knew what we were talking about but me and him knew he gets no ass.

When I got in my truck I called Keisha and told her I was on my way to her house. When I arrived at Keisha's house I had a hand full of roses that I had bought on my way to her house. She smelled them and then gave me a big hug and a kiss. I made my way into the living room and kicked my feet up on her couch like it was my own. I heard her make her way upstairs and I made my play. I stripped all the way down to nothing but my sox. I was gonna be ass naked when she came back down those steps.

Something hit me. I had to make it a little more romantic so I went and grabbed a rose pedal and held it over my dick. Keisha came running down the steps and when she hit the last step she froze, "Yeaaaaaaaaaaa," I said.

We started walking towards each other, met halfway, and then started kissing. Now I know I just went thru a scare but this bitch Keisha had a crazy fat ass. I had to hit this shit raw, fuck the consequences. She started taking her shorts off and I started taking her shirt off. She already knew what time it was. She took a couple of steps towards the couch bent over and looked back at me. It was time to put the murder game down. I slid my dick inside her pussy and started pounding that shit hard and fast. I reached and got my phone and started taking pics and recording this donkey ass.

After going hard for ten minutes the doorbell rang. I ignored it and kept going. "Hold up, Hold up, let me answer the door."

I was in the zone and kept going. I said, "Hold on I'm bout to cum."

After about another thirty seconds I pulled out and came on her ass. She yelled out, "I'm coming," to the person at the door while she ran in the bathroom to wipe the cum off her ass.

When she came out the bathroom she put her shirt, panties, and shorts on and went to answer the door. I was laid out on the couch ass naked dazed thinking about how her fat ass was bouncing back on me. Keisha looked thru the peep hole and panicked. She ran back to me and said, "Hurry up get dressed my boyfriend here."

I said, "Mcfluzieeeee."

This bitch was texting me saying this nigga working both jobs today and this nigga shows up. I got dressed and sat on the couch. She starts walking around in circles tryna get her lying face together. She finally goes up and opens the door. I heard her boyfriend say, "Hey baby, I stopped by on my lunch to come see you."

This nigga tried to come and get a lunch break quickie but little did he know, I just did. I had to find a way out and the only way I knew I could was to act like I was checking something out. I had on a Fire department uniform so this should be easy. "Hey Miss Keisha, I checked out your gas smell in your kitchen and everything checked out. I'm going to check your neighbors and see if they have been smelling gas as well." This nigga looked sold. I walked up to him extended my hand and said, "Hey I'm Todd, and I guess you are the man of the house?"

He gave me a strange look, shook my hand and said, "Good to meet you Todd."

Keisha was messing with a fucking clown; this dude was a straight wigger, a white dude tryna act black. After I walked past them Keisha stopped me and said, "Thanks Chris."

Why the fuck did she just say that? The red flags in this niggas head just went off. I kept it moving. Keisha realized what she had done and tried to close the door. I heard yelling in the house. I was five steps away from my truck when I decided to be Super Save a Hoe. I walked back up to the door and rang the doorbell.

Her boyfriend answered the door and threw the roses I bought at my face. Before I could do anything he caught me with a right hook. I stumbled back, *this nigga was not about to beat my ass.* He started rushing me; I got low and kicked this nigga in his balls. He fell straight

142

to the ground and I went ham on his ass. "Chris stop it's over," yelled Keisha.

I caught him with one last hook to the body and said, "That's my lunch break quickie nigga. Get yo pussy ass up white boy."

I started making my way back to the car and a cop car pulls up. He started walking towards us with his hand on his gun and said, "What's the problem here? I received a call."

I said, "Sir, this thug attacked me."

I knew he would believe me; I had on my Fire Department attire and not to mention this nigga was dressed like a complete thug. "I got it from here," the officer said.

The officer then proceeds to arrest her boyfriend and put him in the car. He tells me not to go anywhere. After he places him in the car he asked me what happened. I told him I was doing Keisha a favor when I was attacked by her boyfriend. The officer asked if I wanted to press charges and I said, "No."

The officer then looked at me and said, "Ok thanks, we are gonna charge him with assault."

This officer just made the decision for me. As the officer was looking down and writing his report I would glance over at Keisha's boyfriend and grill him. That shit pissed him off, I could hear his head beating against the cop car window in anger. Once all the paperwork was filled out I left. I thought about a round two being that this nigga was getting locked up but fuck that. *I just took it in the face for this bitch ain't no way I could stay.*

When I got home I hit Myspace. All I could hear was the lyrics of Tupac going thru my head, *"I ain't no killa but don't push me revenge is like the sweetest joy next to getting pussy."* I logged on Myspace and went to Keisha's page. I scrolled thru her friends and found this clown nigga Kenneth Cutthroat Smith. Typical Myspace name for a fuck boy. I plugged my phone in and uploaded a picture of Keisha's donkey ass. I took the best ass shot of me fucking her and sent it to this niggas inbox.

Subject: *IS THAT YO CHICK?*

Message:

I FUCKED YOU UP AND FUCKED YO BITCH CUH SHE FILE AND YOU WIFED HER.

I showed Jeff and Blow the footage. We played the PlayStation, drank, and talked about what happened all night. I didn't have to work the next morning so I decided I was gonna sleep in. I was woke up by a phone call from Keisha. She was blowing my phone up and I kept hitting ignore and going back to sleep. Finally I answered cranky as hell. I said, "Whatttt?"

I could hear her crying on the other line. From what I could make out of it was, "They let him out of jail."

I said, "Fuck that nigga."

Keisha yelled back at me, "He could be dead."

Now she caught my attention. Keisha went on to tell me that they released him and he came to her house all pissed. He told her about the pictures I sent him and she denied it. After about thirty minutes of arguing he went out to his car and called her begging her to tell the

144

truth. She said she still lied and she heard a gunshot. The phone grew silent. I said, "So what happened?"

Still no answer just her tryna refrain from crying. "He shot himself in the head," she said while crying uncontrollably.

All I could say was Mcfluzie. I knew this nigga was a sucker for love but not like this. I hung up the phone and went in the kitchen to clear my mind. *Was I the cause of this?* Blow was on the couch and said while laughing, "I'ma call that fuck nigga bullet head."

I looked at him and said, "What you talkin bout?"

Blow said, "Shit all on the news, that nigga who bitch you fucked blew his head off and now he in critical condition. He is definitely a sucka for love ass nigga."

Even though I was pissed about what happened I called Keisha and told her to come over my crib. I laid down in my room on my bed staring at the ceiling thinking about everything that led up to him shooting himself. I didn't know how Keisha would respond to being around me now. I heard the doorbell ring and I jumped up. Before I could get to the door Blow answers it. "I'm sorry for your loss; you must have some good pussy to cause a nigga to blow his head off."

I looked at this nigga like I was gonna fuck him up. Keisha ignored him and walked back to my room. When she entered the room she sat beside me and said, "I need to free my mind."

I looked at her smiled and said, "What's that supposed to mean?"

Keshia slid closer to me and said that she wanted to try something new. She leaned in, kissed me and it was on. I stood up and started taking my clothes off and she did the same. After throwing my shirt to the ground I saw something that sparked my imagination. I had handcuffs from a class I had taken with the Fire Department. I walked over to my dresser and picked them up.

Once I had the cuffs in my hand I looked at Keisha laying ass naked on her stomach and said while laughing, "You wanna try something new huh? Well you under arrest for a double homicide."

Keisha played along. I cuffed one of her hands, wrapped the cuffs around one of the bed post, and then cuffed her other hand. Keisha then arched her ass up in the air and I crawled behind her. I slid my dick in and went to work. After about five minutes in Keisha kept screaming for me to put it in her ass. Now I ain't never done that shit before and thinking about doing it made me uncomfortable. I ignored her for a minute till finally I pulled my dick out. Once I did that she arched her back even more. "Put that big dick in my ass," said Keisha.

I grabbed my dick with my right hand and started to force it in her ass hole slowly. Keisha was no amateur at this; she began bouncing back on my dick. This wasn't as bad as I thought it would be. I started pounding her out. Keisha started screaming uncontrollably. After about four minutes I came in her ass. This shit felt nasty as hell I had to go and wash my dick off instantly. As I'm headed to the bathroom I heard fart noises. I was scared to look back. I didn't want to know if it was her pussy or ass. I probably couldn't look at her the same if she was farting out her ass.

After going in the bathroom and washing my dick off I came back in the room and Keisha was out cold still cuffed to my bed. I lie beside her and fell asleep. After being sleep for an hour I felt something hitting my leg. I opened my eyes and Keisha said, "Uncuff me nigga I gotta pee."

I went looking for the key to unlock the handcuffs. I was searching for a good ten minutes. Keisha then began to get worried. To calm her down I said with confidence, "I think it's in the living room."

I threw some shorts and a shirt on and headed into the living room. I see Jeff and Blow playing Madden while sitting on the couch. I walked in front of the TV and said, "Any of y'all know how to unlock handcuffs? Keisha's cuffed to my bed."

These niggas fell off the couch laughing. "Naw nigga I ain't the police," said Jeff.

Blow got up off the floor and started making joke after joke. These niggas were no help. I walked back in the room and I faced the problem head on. I said, "Keisha, I don't have a key to unlock the handcuffs."

Keisha went crazy, "What the fuck you mean nigga? Why would you cuff me with no keys mother fucker? How the fuck I'ma get this shit off?"

I calmly tried to neutralize the situation and said, "We have to call the cops to take them off, there is no other option." I could see Keisha was extremely pissed. I picked up my cellphone and called 911.

The operator asks, "911, what's your emergency?"

I was nervous but I had to be clutch, "Umm I have a lady handcuffed to my bed and we don't have a key to uncuff her."

I just knew the lady on the other line was gonna bust out laughing. She continued to ask me for my address and said that she is sending a patrol car my way. After I hung up I took the covers and put them over Keisha so that nobody could see her nakedness. After about twenty minutes two officers arrived. When they walked in my room they asked how it happened. I began to explain when one of the officers said, "Shut up, I wanna hear her tell me."

Keisha went on to explain what happened and they busted out laughing at the both of us. The officers asked me where I got the cuffs from and I said, "The Fire Department when we took a training course."

One of the officers went to take the handcuffs off. After they were off Keisha balled up under the covers. "If we gotta come out here again for your little sex games we gonna lock both y'all up," said one of the officers.

I responded, "Yes sir thanks for helping."

When we made our way to the front door the other officer says, "Stick to putting out fires leave the handcuffing to us." They both started laughing while walking away.

When I walked back in my room Keisha was getting dressed. After she got everything on she gave me a kiss on the cheek and said her goodbyes. "Damn you just gonna take the dick then leave?"

She ignored me and kept it moving. I wasn't about to chase this bitch so I let her leave. I went in my room and closed the door. After taking another power nap I heard my phone ringing. I answered and it was Keisha. She told me she was at the hospital and her boyfriend was doing better. *I felt some relief but thought how could she just do what we did and go see him. These hoes are heartless.* I had to flip the script on her for leaving my crib like that. "Fuck that nigga and fuck you too," I said.

She started crying and right then I knew I won. "Fuck me? You saying fuck me? You run up in me raw and now its fuck me? Well I guess it's fuck yo child I'm carrying too huh?" My heart dropped and before I could say anything she hung up.

CHAPTER 15
CAUGHT SLIPPIN

"There is no safe way to play with fire. If you play with fire
always be prepared to get burnt."

There was no way that I could have two kids on the
way. My nigga Stretch was on the way here and there
was no way I was gonna allow Keisha to fuck up my
good time. I had to call my nigga Bam and get some
advice. Even though there was allot of bad shit that went
down back in VA involving him. He did try to talk me out
and help me in every situation. Bam was like my good
conscious; I was just too hard headed. We talked about
where I stood with Keisha and how she said that she
was gonna get an abortion.

Bam was all for me assisting her in getting the
abortion and I used him as a mediator between the both

of us. I gave Bam her number to call her and talk some sense in her and it actually worked. He got her to set up a time for the abortion and I was gonna pay for it. Now that the situation was over with it was time to get back to the turn up with another chick on my roster named Whitney aka Midget.

I called her Midget because she really is one literally. Midget had a friend for Stretch and we all was gonna kick it at my house on this Friday night. Midget had two sons one was three and the other five. I'm only 5'3 myself so I didn't really feel bad smashing a Midget and plus her ass was super fat. Imagine Nia Long with Nicki Minaj body but in the form of a Midget. It would tempt anybody to smash. Midget was the type of girl that would give you the clothes off her back and that's what kept her around on my team.

Now Stretch didn't know anything about Midget being a Midget and I knew nothing about how her friend looked. Looks didn't matter anyway for Stretch he doesn't turn down nothing but his collar. Stretch arrived at my house that Friday night at about 7pm. I made sure my roommate Jeff and his freeloading ass cousin Blow were not around. Stretch and I chopped it up and was sippin on some vodka until Midget and her friend arrived around 8pm.

Stretch was feeling nice and was saying some off the wall shit. When I opened the door for Midget and her friend I was shocked, her friend was bad as fuck. I gave her friend a hug and whispered, "You look nice," in her ear. I was definitely gonna try to flip these hoes.

Right after she walked in Midget walks up to me and gives me a kiss. "Bro, that's a Fucking Midget," said Stretch while laughing.

"Yea I'm a Midget and ya boy likes it."

That made it awkward as all hell. I went and got some glasses and poured them some liquor. They were taking that shit to the head. Stretch was already lit so everything he said was direct and reckless. "So let's get this poppin. I know y'all ain't come all the way here to just mingle did y'all?" Midget and her friend didn't say a word. "Let's watch a porno," said Stretch. Again they were silent. Stretch looked at Midget's friend and said, "What's your name?"

She responded, "Alisha."

"Well Alisha would you care to watch some porn?"

Alisha had a smirk on her face, "I'm down for whatever."

"Shrimp go get some pornos I know yo ass got some."

I went in my bedroom and grabbed a DVD. While I was putting it in I said, "Y'all gonna like this its homegrown porn."

Not even three seconds into it playing Stretch yells out, "Yoooooo Shrimp that's you dawg."

I started busting out laughing. Midget was pissed but Alisha was glued to the screen. "I'm ready to go," said Midget.

"What you mad for? It's old porn of me," I said. I got up and cut the TV off.

"Nigga my dick way bigger than yours Shrimp," said Stretch.

"The fuck it is."

"Let's let the girls be the judge," said Stretch. He got up and stood beside me. "Let's pull it out on three. One, Two, and Three," said Stretch as he pulled his dick out.

I had to do the same. It ain't matter to me; Midget already knew what time it was. I pulled my dick out and seen this nigga Stretch looking at my dick with his arms in a field goal position. "And the winner is," said Stretch.

My dick was all soft. "Shrimp you are a grower," said Alisha.

Everyone started laughing. Midget walks up to me and says, "Let me get it hard and then let's judge."

Midget walks over to me gets on her knees, puts my dick in her mouth, and starts sucking it. While she's giving me head Stretch is still standing beside me and starts rubbing his hand across Midget's hair. Midget didn't say a word. I didn't know if I should be mad or what. "This ain't fair, Alisha you gotta get my dick hard now," said Stretch.

Without any hesitation she walks over to Stretch, gets on her knees, jerks his dick a couple of times then begins to suck it. Stretch and I were about to get it in with these bitches. After about five minutes of getting head from Midget she stops and says, "I'm tryna fuck."

I followed Midget into my room and now it was time to lay down the murder game. As I'm taking my clothes off I could hear my phone going off. I ignored it and started kissing Midget as she lay down on my bed.

Midget said, "Ain't you gonna answer?" I ignored her and kept kissing her. She pushed me away. "Go answer yo phone somebody keep calling you," said Midget. I get up and walk to my phone I had eighteen missed calls and three text messages from Bam.

Text Messages

10:45 PM Bam: *Keisha at yo crib pick up Cuh*

10:50 PM Bam: *Pick up nigga this bitch bout to knock yo windows out*

10:55 PM Bam: *This bitch crazy Cuh*

I panicked when I read the text messages. I went and looked out the blinds slowly and there was Keisha looking right at me with a baseball bat in her hand. Immediately I ran in the living room where Stretch and Alisha were. "Mcfluzie," I said. This bitch was riding this nigga Stretch reverse cowgirl, and to make matters worse he was hitting the bitch raw daddy. I walked up to Stretch with no respect for them being naked and said, "I need yo help man this bitch tryna knock my windows out."

Stretch looked at me then looked at Alisha ass while she was bent over bouncing off his dick and just pointed at her ass. Stretch said, "You see this nigga? Nigga, do you see this fat ass bouncing off my dick?"

I said, "C'mon man this is life or death."

Stretch moved Alisha to the side and stood up. I stared at Alisha as she was putting her clothes on. I had to get some of that. Stretch walked up to me with his dick hanging out, put his arm around me, and said, "What is so important that you interrupted me from getting some quality pussy?"

154

I explained to Stretch the situation and he told me exactly what I ain't want to hear. Stretch told me to tell Midget. I had to find out the specifics so I called Bam back. Bam had nothing but bad news for me. Bam said that Keisha saw Midget and Alisha come over and was about to bust my truck windows out until he convinced her otherwise. He said he had to negotiate a happy medium. The happy medium ended up being her slashing one tire and taking the plates off my truck. I was pissed, this bitch got me good. Midget and Alisha must have eased dropped on my whole conversation. They started packing they shit up.

Midget walked past me and I asked her what was wrong. She jumped up and smacked me. I held my face in shock and watched as they walked out the apartment. I knew I was caught, there was no reason for me to chase her, and I knew I could get her back. After Midget slammed the door on the way out this nigga Stretch started laughing uncontrollably. "Nigga, a Midget just jumped and smacked you," said Stretch.

This shit was all funny to him. I looked out the patio window to ensure that Keisha was gone and didn't run up on Midget and Alisha. After the coast was clear I ran out to my truck. The damage was exactly what Bam said it was. My plates were gone and my driver side tire was flat. I had to get this fixed right away because they tow in my neighborhood for shit like this. I went to get my spare tire and changed it out with the flat tire. After I was finished I noticed that there was a note on the windshield.

155

Chris,

You got me pregnant and think you can run around and be a hoe. I got some shit for yo ass. Have fun getting yo shit fixed.

I could have called the police on this bitch. I had all the evidence I needed. I played it smart; I needed to wait until she gets this abortion. When I walked back in my apartment this nigga Stretch was sitting on the couch watching my porno. I was so pissed that he didn't help me. I walked past him and didn't say a word. I decided that I was gonna walk to the corner store to get some milk and on the way call Keisha. As I'm walking out the neighborhood I remembered I needed a plate for my truck. I walked up to a green truck and screwed the plates off. After I got the plates I tucked it in my pants and jogged out the neighborhood.

I called Keisha and she answered on the first ring, she went off. After about ten minutes she finally was able to calm down and talk. I walked in the store still on the phone with Keisha. I got milk and got up out of there. By the time I was headed back to my house she was apologizing for doing that stupid shit. As I'm walking I see a small dude walking past me and he asked me a question. I couldn't really make out what he was saying because I was too busy caking on the phone. I shrugged my shoulders and kept it moving.

As I hit the street to get to my house I hear someone behind me say, "Don't fucking turn around or I'ma blow yo fucking head off."

I froze and put my hands in the air. I tried to get a glance at who it was, before I could partially get my head around one of the guys pistol whipped me. I fell to the ground face first and someone pressed their shoe on the back of my head. "I dare you to fucking move again," one of the guys said.

I lay there motionless while they ran my pockets and took my cellphone. Whoever had their foot on my head moved it and I felt someone pour milk all over me. I was still lying there too scared to move. They were kicking me in my ribs, stomping me on my back, and then I heard them running away.

I laid there face down for a couple of minutes. I lifted my head up and didn't see anyone in site. I got up and ran home as fast as I could. Once I made it in the living room I yelled out, "I got robbed."

With milk all over me I laid out on the floor. I was in tears mostly because of my adrenaline. Stretch asked me what happened and I told him. I could tell he wanted to make jokes but he didn't. I went in my room, closed the door and went to sleep.

I woke up the next morning and I had two things on my agenda. Get me a new phone and go with Keisha to get the abortion. As I walked out my room I seen Blow and Stretch playing Madden while sitting on the couch. Blow said, "Got Milk?" These niggas couldn't stop laughing. "Welcome to Baltimore fool," said Blow.

I started getting dressed and ready to head out; I had to meet Keisha at 3 o'clock. I dapped Stretch up and told him it was nice seeing him again and headed out. I went and got a new phone and made it to the clinic around 2:30pm. I texted Keisha to let her know I was there. It was 3pm and still I received no response from her. I started blowing her phone up and she still was not answering.

Finally, I went to the desk gave the lady Keisha name, and told her what I was here for. The lady said that there was never an appointment scheduled. I was pissed. I got back in my truck and sat there for about an hour calling her and still no answer. I started texting her every letter in the alphabet and pressing send. After making it through the alphabet two times I received a call from her. I answered and said, "Why you playing damn games?"

I got a response back but it wasn't from Keisha. "This is Officer James with Baltimore County Police Department you need to stop harassing this young lady," said the guy on her phone.

"She stood me up for an abortion how am I harassing her?"

"All I know is she is pressing charges and you need to stop contacting her."

I hung up the phone. I had to take my mind off this bullshit so I decided to call Midget and try to finish what I started. After about twenty minutes of convincing her she finally gave in. I went to go pick her up and headed to my crib. Once we arrived it was on. With my bad luck my phone was ringing off the hook again. "It's prolly one of yo hoes again," said Midget.

I went to answer my phone when it rang again and it was my baby mom's. I said, "What you want?"

Her Mom responded, "What you mean what I want? She is going into labor fool."

I got the hospital information from her and hung up the phone. I didn't even have to explain to Midget what was going down she heard every word. I didn't have time to take Midget home and plus I was riding hot with a doughnut. I called a cab for Midget and headed to the hospital.

When I made it to the hospital I saw my baby mom's family outside of the room and they all signaled me to go in. As I walked in the room I saw my son in my baby mom's arms. My whole life flashed in front of my eyes. I now felt like I had a purpose and I had to provide a way for someone else. I held him in my arms and tears began running down my face. It was time to leave these other chicks alone. I had a son now and he comes first.

CHAPTER 16
HIT AND RUN

"When you are labeled a bad guy you might sometimes think you won because the good guys always finish last."

Having a newborn child would change a lot of people and for me it did. After being in the hospital for four days I settled in at my baby mom's house. I enjoyed being around my son but it was torture. I couldn't have sex with my baby mom's so there was really no purpose for me to be here other than my son. I decided to call a chick named April I met while at work running a call.

April talked a good game. She was in school to be a nurse and she had her life all planned out. April played that hard to get shit. I was only able to smash one time a while ago. I know I could have called around 10-15 girls and the pussy would be on demand but I'm to the point now where I'm starting to enjoy the chase. We talked on the phone for hours on the front porch at my baby mom's house and made plans to meet up the next day and chill.

After I got off the phone I walked back in the house and people handshakes wasn't matching they smile. I asked my baby mom's brother if he wanted to play Madden and he turned me down. Something wasn't right. After sitting on the couch for about ten minutes someone broke the ice. My baby mom's mother said, "I hope you not a deadbeat. Chasing these fast girls out here and being with my daughter ain't acceptable." I gave her the dumb look and said, "With all due respect, I haven't been a father for a week yet. It's too early to call me a deadbeat Dad especially when I'm here with my son."

My sarcasm wasn't taken well by her. She stood up and said, "Get the fuck out my house and go lay up with that bitch you was whispering sweet nothings to on the phone."

I smirked, stood up, looked at my son and said, "Bye son, I will see you soon," as I started walking out the door.

When I made it to the door my baby mom's mother started running after me. I turned around when I saw her running and started walking backwards down the porch steps. I said, "What's your problem? You are acting like a damn kid."

That really pissed my baby mom's mother off. She lunged towards me, threw a hook and I blocked it. I looked at her and my baby mom's and said, "Really? You tryna fight me?"

They all looked at me like this shit was acceptable. My baby mom's brother took a step towards me and said, "You better not put yo hands on my moms."

Those words from her son gave her confidence to believe that it was now 2 vs 1. She rushed me and started throwing punches and I was deflecting all of them. I had to protect myself and I did so the only way I knew how without punching this bitch in the face. I let her get tired while she continued to throw flurries of punches and then I made my move. I ducked real low, took a step to the side, grabbed her around her legs, and dumped her right on her fucking neck.

As soon as I released her into the ground I took off running. My baby mom's brother tried to chase me but only took five steps and stopped. There is no nigga in America that is gonna chase after a nigga after they seen someone get taken for the ride of their life like that.

I ran out of their site and waited until they went in the house to examine their Mom then I ran to my truck. As I tried to start the truck up I was fumbling the keys, I was nervous as shit. Finally I got the car started and pulled off. I could see my baby mom's mother and her brother chasing my car out the driveway. As I hit the corner I stuck my middle finger up out the window. The bridge with my baby mom's family was officially burnt. There was no way I could dump someone's Mom on her neck and we could ever be cool.

162

After making it home, I laid down on my bed, called April and pillow talked. She was telling me about all the shit she wanted me to do to her. It made me horny as shit. I started beating my dick while I was on the phone and if she wasn't playing with herself on the other line then she needed a fucking Oscar. We stayed on the phone all night until we fell asleep. The next morning it was time to get it in. Where she stayed at in Baltimore was rough so I asked Blow to ride with me. This nigga loved getting into shit so he agreed and we headed out there to see her.

I wanted to give April that surprise dick. I wanted to knock on her door and catch her when she had nothing on but booty shorts and a shirt. I got out the truck, walked up to April's door and knocked. She came to the door fully dressed. I leaned in to get a hug from her and she kissed me on my lips. I said, "So what's good? I'm tryna see if you bout that life."

April smiled and said, "Me too but I have to take my Mom to a doctor appointment." I explained to her that I was trying to surprise her and she said I should have called her first and she will be home later that day. I agreed to come back at 8pm that night, she would have taken her Mom home by then and we would have the whole night to ourselves.

We said our goodbyes and I headed back to my truck. When I opened the truck door I could see the weed smoke. Blow was in the truck getting shell as a bitch. Blow asked why I ain't go in and I told him. He started laughing and said, "Another nigga prolly coming over." I decided to hit the blunt he was smoking. As I pulled off I reached my hand over to him for the blunt, "Shrimp you smoking tree now? Shit this bitch must got some good pussy." As I inhaled the smoke I coughed, I haven't smoked in forever. Blow said, "You gotta pop that cherry again virgin lungs."

We laughed as I continued to drive off. I don't know if it was the weed or what but something told me to stakeout April's crib, I had to put her to the faithful test. I rode around to the adjacent neighborhood and parked. I now had a clear view of April's house. Blow said, "What we doing nigga? We can't be sitting out here like this, you asking to get robbed."

I told Blow that I had to see if this bitch was really faithful. As we sat with the seats back blowing down the blunt I saw April come out the house and get into a silver Ford Taurus. It was the same car that was parked down the street when I pulled up. I sat up in my seat and to no surprise Blow was already glued in on the action.

We sat there and watched her sit in the car with some nigga and it looked like they were mad cool with each other. I started calling her phone to see if she would answer and it went straight to voicemail. I started the truck up and started speeding towards this bitch. April had me come all the way out here to Mcfluzie me with some fuck nigga. As I'm entering the neighborhood I heard Blow talking to himself saying how he was gonna fuck this nigga up.

When I got in April's neighborhood I parked in front of the Taurus and got out. I walked up to the passenger side and Blow walks up on the driver side where old boy was. Blow punches the window, "Get the fuck out the car shawty."

The dude was scared shitless, he put his hands up and started saying he ain't want no problems. I kept pulling on the door handle telling April to get the fuck out the car and she wouldn't. Blow yelled out to the dude in the car, "Unlock the doors before I break yo damn face shawty."

The dude reached quick and hit the unlock button. Blow opened the door grabbed dude by his collar and yoked him out the car onto the ground. Blow told dude not to fucking move. I opened April's door and started cussing her ass out. She started crying and apologizing and I wasn't tryna hear that shit. I said, "You are a fucking hoe bitch. You had me come all the way out here and you fucking with these punk lame ass niggas?"

I was heated almost to the point I was about to choke her but I seen something much more valuable. I grabbed her phone and started running back to my truck. Blow saw me and ran too. Once we got in the truck I started it, and before I knew it April was at my window. I looked at April and said, "Since you wasted my time I'ma waist yours."

I continued to drive away and April punched me in my face. She continued to lunge herself into my truck and reach for her phone. I sped up and started swerving. April kept trying to punch me while I was driving and I tried to push her back out the window. Finally I wedged her away and she fell. I heard a thump. Blow said, "Pull off we done ran the bitch over."

I tossed her phone out the window and peeled off. When we made it back to the crib Blow couldn't stop talking about me running the bitch over. Blow kept saying, "Y'all VA Niggas wild. Y'all running bitches over."

I was tired of all the bullshit that was going on. I had to get my life right it seemed like I'm always getting caught up in some shit. That whole weekend I stayed in the house and rested up knowing I had to go back to work in two days. The next day I woke up at around

165

3pm. I picked my phone up and noticed I had two text messages.

Text Messages

1:05 PM April: Yo *ass is going to jail I filed a police report on yo dumb ass.*

1:20 PM April: *oh and I forgot you got a warrant*

Mcfluzie! This bitch was a real live snitch. I jumped up off the bed, ran in the living room to get on the computer to see if I had a warrant. Blow was lying on the couch watching TV. I said, "Get up, I got a damn warrant."

Blow sat up and said, "What else you thought was gonna happen you ran a bitch over."

This shit was funny to Blow but this was my life. I logged into the computer typed my name in and show nuff I had warrants. Not only did I have a warrant from the April incident but another one for harassment of Keshia. I got up walked to the couch and sat down. I was holding back tears. *I knew I was innocent but the court wouldn't see it that way. To them I was just another Baltimore thug.*

I looked at Blow and said, "Take me to turn myself in."

Blow looked at me all while laughing and said, "Nigga you ain't turning shit in, you are officially on the run. My Nigga."

CHAPTER 17

BIND

"When you are in a bind you will see who your real friends are."

I tried to keep a clear mind. I knew if I called Keisha it would only make matters worse. I figured that I would use the out of sight out of mind mentality and maybe everything would be ok. I got dressed and headed into work. The thoughts of becoming a real family with my baby mother actually was possible. As I hit the highway I noticed a police car cruising behind me. Being that I had a warrant there was no way I could let him get behind me and read my plates.

I switched lanes and slowed down trying to let the officer get as far ahead as possible. Looking straight not trying to make eye contact, I saw the officer slow down and allow me to get in front. I felt like taking this dude on a high speed chase. After driving for about five minutes the cop hit his lights. I pulled over to the side of the road scared as shit. I sat in my truck for a good ten minutes until the officer came up to my door. The officer said, "Do you know why I pulled you over son?"

I was about to say because I have a warrant and just get it over with but I figured since I had on my Fire Department uniform I could talk my way out of it. I said, "Possibly speeding sir, I had to get to the firehouse to relieve someone else that's been on duty and I'm running late."

The officer looked at me and said, "I appreciate what you do but can you explain to me why you have stolen tags on your vehicle?"

I paused, I had completely forgotten that I stole those tags off someone else's car. I got myself together and said, "I let my girlfriend use my car I'm just getting back in town I'm sure they are a friend of hers."

The officer then asked for my license and registration and said, "If everything checks out I'll have to take the plate, write you a ticket, and I'll get you on your way."
I asked, "How am I supposed to drive with no tags?"
The officer responded, "I'ma let you go without towing you just consider it a thanks for service." He began to chuckle and said, "Now if anyone else pulls you over then it's up to them to do whatever."

I handed the officer my license and registration and he began to check everything out in his car. I was sweating bullets. The officer was in his car for about twenty minutes. Out of nowhere I saw two other cop cars speed up and the officers hopped out with their hands on their guns. The officer that pulled me over then gets out with his gun drawn and asks me to step out the truck with my hands up. I opened the door and stuck both my hands out first. I was not about to be another black guy falling victim to police brutality. I put my feet out and stood up. The officers then asked me to turn around and put my hands on my head slowly. After doing so I was rushed by the officer that pulled me over, slammed on the hood of my truck and handcuffed.

The officer said that I was under arrest and that I had two warrants one for felony hit and run and the other harassment. The officer started reading me my rights but took it too personal, "You had the right to hit and run and we have the right to fuck you up," one of the officers said.

I felt like shit. After they read me my rights the officer that pulled me over threw me in his squad car. I noticed they never patted me down. I could have had a gun and killed one of these pigs. As I was moving around in the back of the car one of the officers noticed it and came over to the driver's side door. He reached in and said, "Why you keep fucking moving around back there? I'm gonna make you real comfortable."

I thought he was gonna hit me or some shit but this pussy ass officer turned the heat on blast. This must be a torture tool all cops use. I couldn't breathe for shit. I kept breathing out my nose with my mouth closed slowly. Finally after the officer came back in I said, "Yea I know your fat ass ain't gonna drive with this heat on."

The officer quickly turned the A/C on and said, "Look man, I'm not the enemy I was going to let you go but I can't ignore a fucking warrant. Two warrants at that."

The whole ride the officer tried to have friendly conversations but fuck that shit, any nigga locking me up ain't never cool in my book. I was first taken to the Baltimore City Jail where I was immediately booked. I was in a room with two bunk beds. The so called mattress had no cushion but was the only thing protecting me from the infested floor. There was a toilet in the middle of the room. *How was I gonna take a shit in front of other niggas?* I was in there with another nigga who had been picked up for a DWI. The dude name was Mecho and seemed mad cool. Mecho was from Jersey and had just moved to Baltimore County. He kept asking me what was going to happen next because he has never been locked up before like I could really answer those questions.

After a couple hours of sitting talking about our cases, we were both taken to the Baltimore County Jail. When we got there I had to change and then wait in a room with benches where myself, Mecho, and about twelve other dudes had to sit. Next we had to wait until a holding cell was available and then go to the bonding hearing to possibly bail out. Everyone was quiet and to themselves except four niggas that was playing spades. I walked up to the table and said, "Me and my partner Mecho got next."

I may have got my ass whipped in VA, but one thing I do know is I dodged a lot of ass whooping's by approaching situations aggressive. A real nigga will not go through the headache of fucking with a real nigga. One of the niggas at the table said, "Shawty where you from?"

I said, "I'm from VA Beach."

They all grew quiet. "It's some real niggas in VA. I know some cats named Monty, Jackal and Wolf from out Hampton."

These dudes were as real as it gets. They gave me advice on my case and we talked about VA, Baltimore, and hood politics. They asked me what part of Baltimore I was living in and I told them I stayed out Dove Landing Apartments. "Say word? Nigga that's my hood," said one of the guys named Broski.

The other niggas at the table was talking shit saying if he was a big dawg then I would have heard about him if we lived in the same hood. That shit made Broski mad. He started telling stories about how he be selling dope and putting in work. He had mad niggas laughing. He started telling a story on how if you walked through his block and he ain't know you he would rob you. He said one night he was chillin with his niggas at the corner store and saw some lame ass nigga on the phone arguing with his girl. He said he walked pass the nigga and asked him if he wanted to buy some tree and the nigga just waved him off.

Broski said that pissed him off and it made the dude a soft target. Being that he had this new HTC phone he was gonna rob him. He said they ran across the street while dude was in the store and posted up on a car out the neighborhood. He saw the dude walk by still on the phone with milk in his hand. Broski ran up behind the nigga and said, "Don't turn around or Ima blow yo fucking head off."

Broski said, "The nigga pissed his pants, shit was running all down his legs." Everyone was laughing they ass off, this nigga really knew how to tell a story. Broski then went on to say he pistol whipped the nigga and the nigga fell. After he fell Broski said they started stomping the dude and the dude was praying out loud for Jehovah to save him. Broski said after he ran the dude pockets he took his HTC phone and said to the dude, "Jehovah said he wants me to baptize you." He said his homeboys thought he was gonna shoot the nigga but he reached for the gallon of milk. He said he poured the milk all on the nigga then they hauled ass. Everyone was crying laughing except me; I knew the nigga that was covered in milk was me.

At first I thought I should wait til this nigga sleep, sneak him and beat this nigga ass. I thought these other niggas would probably help him so I had to control my anger and play along. I didn't want to be in here any longer then needed and I knew if I fought him I would be a target around here. After about an hour, I was finally taken to a holding cell. It was one of three available at that time. The cells were not that wide and each had about twelve dudes in there. There were only four mats for us to share and a toilet. The water fountain did not work, so we could only drink when a meal was brought to us.

With our meal we were given a small ass sized milk and one gulp sized cup of fruit punch. We got that three times a day and that is all we had to drink. I stayed in the holding cell for another five hours until I was finally booked and printed. Once we were booked we all were allowed to use the phone. I was nervous as shit. There was no way I could have called my parents. I called Stretch, He said, "You fucking idiot Shrimp. What the Fuck did you do?"

I was too drained to explain all that could come out of my mouth was, "Mcfluzie, the bitch done got me dawg."

I told Stretch to stay by his phone and I would call him later. Before I hung up Stretch said, "Hold up, Aye man be safe I love you."

I don't know if he thought it was that type of party in here like you see on TV but I never heard a man say that to me before. Stretch and I were like brothers so I guess that's why he cared so much. Next, I figured I would call Bam and ask him what to do in my situation being he has been in my shoes before.

Bam answered on the second ring, "Mcfluzie! I see you getting your feet wet in Baltimore."

I was pissed by his little bullshit joke but began picking his brain. This nigga was no help at all. He would give me advice then start talking about some bitches he got. That's the last thing I wanted to hear at this point. I hung up and called Blow. Now Blow wasn't a very smart nigga but when it came to crime and doing time this nigga had connections. Blow said he knew a bail bondsman that could look out for me and said that he would call to set everything up after my bond hearing. I gave him my parents number to call and brief them in case my bail was too much for me or I couldn't post bail. After that another five hours went by before I was taken before the judge for bonding. I was given a fifty thousand dollar bond.

When we were done, we returned to the cells where I remained another eight hours until I was taken into the room to make another phone call. I called Blow and told him about my situation but he already knew.

173

Blow told me that he told my parents everything and put them in contact with the bail bondsman. This niggas was the last person you want telling your parents that you locked up. My parents probably thought they were talking to an inmate. Blow came through though; he told me that my parents were going to put up the 10% they charged on my bail so I could get out.

I was shocked; I thought my parents would have completely turned their backs on me. After getting off the phone with Blow I decided to call Midget. I wanted her to pick me up from the bail bondsman. Midget answered on the fourth ring, "Oh my god what are you doing in jail?"

I told her about Keisha and tried to put the blame on her. I told her I wouldn't have ever gotten locked up for tricking on the hoes if she wouldn't have walked out and stayed by my side. Midget agreed to pick me up and asked for my parents info because she was going to help them out if needed.

When I hung up the phone I stood there dazed, this chick is really a rider. I was taken back to the cells. I waited there again for about six hours until I was taken back into the room with benches and waited for my turn to leave. After sitting in the room for two and a half more hours, I was finally given my clothes and property back then released. After I left, I had to go across the street to the bonding agency that had bailed me out. I spent another hour in there. I had to check in weekly until my case was filed as dropped. As I'm getting the Dog the Bounty Hunter lecture from the bail bondsman Midget walked in.

I was sitting in the chair and she walks up in between my legs and gives me a kiss. "Promise me you never go back again and you gonna leave these other hoes alone," said Midget.

I looked at her in her eyes kissed her again and said, "I Promise."

I knew that I wasn't going back to jail but the part about leaving these hoes alone was not going to happen. My phone was dead so I asked Midget to use her phone. I had to call my job ASAP. They picked up on the first ring and the fucking square answered the phone. I started explaining that I was in the hospital and he said, "Cut the bullshit you've been in jail and you are no longer employed here."

I was pissed; this nigga must be looking at the jail intake site every day waiting for a nigga to fuck up. I could have called my union rep or my supervisor but I fucked up. There was no way around it. Right when I handed the phone to Midget it rung. Midget looked at it and said. "It's your Mom."

I answered and my Mom said, "Baby, Christopher are you ok?"

I was not in the mood to explain. "Mom thanks for being there I love you and I'm innocent."

After a moment of silence she says, "I love you too," and we hang up.

A mother knows her son best and she knew I needed time alone. Being in jail is so stressful and unhealthy; my body was covered with rashes by the time I got out. I couldn't tell you what a great feeling it was to step into the shower. After getting out the shower I dried off and laid beside Midget on my bed watching TV. I was laying in comfort in what seemed like a paralyzed state. Midget removed the towel off me and began giving me head. I lay back almost falling asleep. I dozed off and was awakened to Midget standing over me ass naked. She squatted down opened the Trojan wrapper with her mouth and slid the condom on with her mouth. She then grabbed my dick with her hand and slid my dick in her pussy. Midget was riding the shit out of me in what looked like she was jumping up and down on my dick.

After I came she lay on my chest and within minutes I was knocked out. I woke up later that evening to the sounds of loud music and Madden. I went in the bathroom to take a piss and then headed into the living room area. The whole living room was filled with smoke, "Look at this Nigga here," said Blow.

We embraced each other with a hug and we sat there talking about my jail experience. After about ten minutes of talking I realized Midget was gone. *Where the fuck was Midget at?* I headed to my room and all I saw was her bite size thong lying on my bed. I seen my phone on my dresser and when I picked it up I noticed I had some unread text messages.

Text Messages

3:45pm Midget: *I really enjoyed my time with you. Hopefully you learned that these other hoes ain't worth it. I will always be here for you see you soon.*

4:25pm Baby M: *you are a piece of shit of a father you fight my mom and then you get arrested and go to jail you will never see your son again you piece of shit.*

CHAPTER 18
LOOSE ENDS

"Sometimes in life you have to realize which tunnels have no light at the end of them."

I've been working on my relationship with my baby mom's. From the looks of it I am going to have to put in a lot of work. I been talking with Keisha and I got her to agree to drop the charges but with that came a lot of sacrifice. I agreed to try to work out a relationship with Keisha to get back in so she could drop the charges. Keisha and I had planned on getting up today and I can't lie, I kinda did missed her; she was a stone cold freak.

Her ex Bullet Head was now out of the picture. Any nigga that would try to blow his own head off in her eyes would blow his girlfriend's head off too. I helped her see that clearly. You can call me a hater or pillow talker but I did whatever I had to do to win the championship and get the charges dropped. When I made it to Keisha's house she had on nothing but a long t-shirt with a thong underneath. Once I walked in she gave me a big hug and I squeezed her ass as I wrapped my arms around her. I walked over to the couch and sat down as she came and sat beside me.

All that bullshit she did to me was water under the bridge. I couldn't stop thinking about how good she looked and what I was about to do to her. As she started talking about her job and all types of other shit I leaned in and kissed her. She seemed a bit shocked at first but that didn't last long. She reached for my shirt and started taking it off. Once my shirt was off she lay back on the couch and gave me a sexy ass look as she bit her bottom lip. I stood up unbuckled my pants and striped all the way down to nothing. I pulled her thong off got on top of her and started kissing her. She then reached down grabbed my dick and tried to slide it in her pussy.

I stood up and said, "Turn yo ass over," in a very demanding voice. She turned over quick and arched her ass in the air. I slid my dick in and started to go to work. She was moaning like she hasn't had the D in years. I took one of my legs off the couch. I put my left foot on the floor while keeping my right knee on the couch and started going even deeper and faster. I felt myself about to cum and I said to her, "I'm about to cum, turn over so I can cum on your face." With the quickness she jumps up gets on her knees and started beating my dick waiting for me to cum on her face.

I came and her face was screwed up like she was in the pool and somebody splashed water in her face. After I was done she got up, ran in the bathroom, and

178

washed her face off. When she returned to the living room I was getting dressed. Keisha looked at me with a sad face and said, "Where you going so fast?"

I started making my way to the door and said, "We can't be together anymore but it was good while it lasted."

Keisha was enraged. She reached for her shirt put it on and said in a real slow and crazy voice, "So you came over here and used me like I'm some fucking hoe?"

"No, it just hit me, I'm not interested."

Keisha started itching towards the kitchen. "You tell me you love me and you wanna be together. You fucked me raw, came on my face, and now you wanna leave?"

I started opening the door in an attempt to make an escape route. Keisha reached for some knives she had on the kitchen counter. She we so mad she fumbled them. I began to take off. I ran out slammed the door and after taking about three steps I heard the knives hit the door. I started sprinting even faster to my truck. When I got in and started the truck up I saw this chick with a knife in her hand still coming. There was no way that I would be able to back out and drive forward. I hit reverse and started steering my way out the neighborhood backwards.

Once she was out of sight I spun around hit the truck in drive and headed home. This bitch deserved to feel like a hoe. I wanted her to feel the pain I felt when I was locked up. When I got home Jeff and Blow were chillin and talking in the kitchen. I said, "Yoooo, I done got the bitch Keisha back."

They both looked at me and Blow said, "Don't tell me you killed the bitch."

I started laughing and said, "Naw, I killed the pussy, came on her face, and after I was done I said I didn't wanna be with her anymore."

Jeff looked at me and all he could say was, "Mcfluzie."

I then went into details and told them how she chased me with knives and I whipped my way out of there. Blow was quiet the whole time. He was up to something. Finally he spoke, "Yo, We should do April the same way." I didn't understand what he meant by we. Blow then said, "I look way better than the nigga she was with that day, and you already hit her up so let's run a train."

This was the best idea I ever heard this nigga come up with. Jeff said, "Nigga that's the dumbest shit I ever heard. You just went to jail for running this bitch over and now you wanna run a train?"

At this point Jeff's advice was just hate to us. We got up went into the living room and Blow said, "Call the bitch."

I pulled out my phone and called her not knowing what to say. After about four rings she answered, "What you want Shrimp?"

I paused for a second and said, "I missed you girl, I went to jail for you cause I can't see you with nobody else."

April was quiet for a second then in her ghetto ass voice said, "You sure don't act like it. I'm sorry you had to go to jail and all but."

Before she could finish I cut her off and said, "Say no more I'm on the way."

It was risky but worth the try. April said, "Well, I guess you can come over."

Just to make sure she was serious I said, "You ain't gon have no other niggas there are you?"

April laughed and said, "I'm home alone."

I put the phone to my side and did the Tiger Woods celebration. After I finished I put the phone back to my ear and said while trying to be calm, "Ok I'm on my way." After I hung up I said out loud, "That's what you call a motherfuckin playa."

Jeff and Blow had bitter looks on their faces. "Don't tell me u hatin now too, Nigga you told me to call," I said.

Blow gave me a sour look and said, "Nigga you set yourself up, you a dirty nigga."

I started laughing and explained to Blow that you can't outright tell a bitch we runnin a train on her.

Blow stood up and said, "True, true, my nigga you smart. I wasn't even thinking."

At that moment I saw why this nigga got the bail bondsman on speed dial. We hopped in my whip and headed over to April's crib. On the way there we were discussing different ways to set it up. This nigga Blow was mad hyped. We arrived at April's crib and I told Blow just follow my lead. I get to the door and April answered. I peeped my head in and said, "You ain't setting a nigga up are you?"

April started laughing and said, "Naw chill." She looked at me crazy and said, "What the fuck he doing here?"

I decided I would break the ice. "You know how y'all niggas do on this side of Baltimore, I had to make sure you ain't have any goons here."

We all went in and sat down on the sectional she had in the living room. She had candles burning and R&B music playing real low. I noticed she was sitting far away and said, "Why you sitting all the way over there?" She came close to me and laid in my arms. I started gripping her ass and looking at Blow like it's about to go down.

I started kissing on her neck and all I could hear her say was, "ewww baby you gotta stop." I slid my hand up her shirt and started massaging her nipples and the ewwws turned into moans." She said, "You better stop before your friend gets a show."

I saw Blow's body sink into the couch when she said that. I laid April down on her back, lifted her shirt, and started sucking on her breasts and nipples. I began to slide her shorts off as I eased down from her nipples to kissing on her stomach. I slid my jeans off and once I got her shorts off I reached in my pocket for a condom. I ripped it open with my mouth quickly and slid it on my dick. I continued to suck on April's nipples and I felt her squeeze my ass and say, "Put it in."

I moved her panties to the side and slid my dick in. I started stroking her pussy slowly. April gave me a look like she was unfazed by Big Brother Thunder. I went to lift her legs up so I could go to work and I saw this nigga Blow on the couch with his tongue out like a dog beating his dick. I looked away like I didn't see it and began crushing the pussy.

April started reaching for shit that wasn't there, she couldn't take it. I felt like something was hovering over top of me. It was Blow standing over top of April face with his pants down beating his dick. I started stroking the pussy faster and harder trying to bust before he fucked this up for me. Blow squats down and smacks his dick on April's lips and I thought it was all over. "Put that big dick in my mouth," said April.

I was shocked as all hell. April was a fucking thirst bucket. Blow started fucking her mouth harder than I was fucking her pussy. After about five minutes of G banging April. Blow pulled a condom out his pocket signaling he wanted to fuck next. I got up took my condom off and threw it on the floor. I pulled her by the hand instructing her to suck my dick. April got on her knees laid in between my legs and started giving me head. I laid my head back on the couch and stared into the ceiling daydreaming. I felt April's teeth clench down on my dick and I leant up looking down at my dick. Blow was hitting this bitch from the back. He had one hand recording her and pulling her hair with the other. I looked at Blow and said, "Slow down nigga she biting my dick."

This nigga was super thirsty. April took her mouth off my dick for a second and said, "Fuck me harder."

April knew not what she did. This nigga Blow went hard for another minute and came all over her back. I had to jump up. April went into the bathroom and was in there for at least ten minutes. I thought she was in there crying or some shit. When she came out she looked at Blow and said, "You could have stayed home for all of that one minute shit."

We busted out laughing and Blow got up and was thinking of something to say but couldn't say anything. April walked up to Blow kissed him on the lips and said, "It was ok though, just not better than Shrimp."

We laughed and joked for another five minutes and then we headed out. Blow gave her another kiss on the lips. I gave her a hug and whispered in her ear, "You gotta get those charges dropped."

After a kiss on the cheek April said, "I got you boo; just don't bring the minute man next time."

Blow started walking to the truck as April and I still were laughing at the joke. The whole car ride was quiet. Blow kept playing back the video over and over again. Once we got in the house Jeff was on the couch playing Madden. I made sure I was the first to say something. I looked at Blow and said, "Aye, how long is that video a minute long?"

I fell out laughing on the floor. It took Jeff about a couple of minutes to catch on after I kept joking but when he got it he was laughing harder than me. After we stopped laughing uncontrollably I said, "Aye Blow, tell him how my dick taste too."

The room was quiet then Jeff said, "Blow you kissed the bitch after she sucked Shrimp dick?"

Blow looked at Jeff with a puzzled face. Jeff looked at me. I looked back at Jeff and we both fell out laughing uncontrollably. Blow was pissed, I figured it was enough joking for the day. I headed in my room and lay on the bed just thinking about life. *I had to get my life together. I had to do what I had to do to get these chicks to cooperate and it's all over now. I have a son and baby mom's. It was like something got a hold of me. I had to make this family thing happen.* I called up my baby mom's. She answered on the first ring, "You fucking dead beat. What the fuck you want?"

I let her continue her rant until finally I said, "Look here. I love you and my son. I want both of y'all to have the best, and I will stop at nothing to make sure you do." My baby mom's grew quiet. I thought long and hard before I spoke again and then I said, "I'm coming to get you and my son to come live with me. We are going to be a family and live our life right according to Jehovah."

CHAPTER 19

CHANGE

"People always talk about change but sometimes it's best to just do it then say it."

It seemed like my life was on the right track. I moved my baby mom's in, and found another job working with a patient transportation company. That feeling of coming home to a good home cooked meal every day and spending family time was the best ever. I had completely cut all of these Baltimore hoes off but my past was still a problem. Today I had to go to court for the hit and run with April and it could end with me being locked up. My baby mom's was non supportive due to the fact it involved another chick so I decided to get Blow to roll with me.

Once I made it to the courtroom the DA asked for everyone to say guilty or non-guilty when they call your name, and to say the last name of your attorney. When they got to me I said out loud, "Not guilty, Shutter."

My lawyer was a cool young white dude with slick brown brushed back hair. After about ten minutes I felt a tap on my shoulder and Mr. Shutter whispered in my ear, "Come with me for a second to discuss your case." I got up and tapped Blow to follow me. We walked out of the courtroom and into a conference room that was next door. As Blow and I sat down I realized that the look on Mr. Shutter's face meant I was about to get some bad news.

Mr. Shutter began to tell us that the DA won't drop the charges because of April saying she is fearing for her life and safety. It felt like my heart fell out my chest. I said in a low voice, "So how much time am I looking at?"

Mr. Shutter looked and said, "If you take the plea to a lesser charge you are looking at one to three years."

I almost cried. Blow stood up in anger and said, "That bitch lying, we both fucked her at the same time after this happened."

Mr. Shutter said, "Calm down young man. If we had proof then it would be a different story, but these are just accusations."

Blow said, "I got the shit on my phone nigga."

Blow began to power his phone on and find the video. Once he located it he handed the phone to Mr.

Shutter. Mr. Shutter's face grew in amazement. He said, "So this happened after you got out of jail?"

Blow responded, "Yes nigga."

Mr. Shutter stood up and said, "I'ma show this to the DA and I'll be right back."

After about ten minutes he returned and said that they are rescheduling the court date to talk to April and review more evidence. Mr. Shutter then began to say that April was a no show and that could be good for the case. After getting back home and playing with my son I realized, my son could not grow up here in Baltimore after all I been through. I sat my baby mom's down and told her that I would be moving her and my son to North Carolina with my parents until I got situated with this court situation.

I thought she was going to take it the wrong way but she actually agreed. A couple of weeks passed and my baby mom's was settled in with my son at my parents crib. They were going to service faithfully and it seemed like life was headed in the right direction. There was still one thing I couldn't shake and it was the women.

I met this chick named Nasonte aka Panama on Myspace right after my baby mom's left. Panama had a Caramel skin complexion, green eyes, was built like Draya, and had an accent like Rihanna. I couldn't tell you if it was her accent or her beauty but I was gone like Pookie in New Jack city. Panama was married to some dude in Norfolk VA that was in the military and they separated, she wanted a new start. Me being the sucka for love that I am I agreed to let her stay with me. I introduced her to Bam and Stretch over the phone and they both consigned.

Panama was supposed to come up tomorrow for the weekend, drop some stuff off, and come back up that following weekend for good. Stretch wanted to come so bad that it made me think he wanted Panama but I paid it no mind. Stretch and I set the rules long ago we don't mess with wifey. When Stretch and Panama arrived I walked straight to Panama. This bitch was super bad. I gave her a hug with my hand on her ass and just seen this nigga Stretch looking with hate.

We headed straight to my room. Before I could close the door Stretch called my name and said, "I'ma have company over soon."

I completely ignored his last attempt to cock block. When we made it into the room I began kissing her. "Let me take a shower," she said.

I completely ignored her. After taking our clothes off I smelt an odor. I went to put my dick in as I was on top of her. As I reached down I was hit with another strong odor. I took it as this chick been driving long and just needed to shower. I continued to proceed and slid my dick in. After going in for about ten minutes, I pulled out and lay on my back for her to get on top. Panama climbed on top and started moving like a white girl. I grabbed her ass and started gunning her pussy. I started to tense up and said in a low voice, "I'm bout to cum."

Panama jumped up and started sucking my dick as I was cumin. I laid there afterwards just paralyzed. Panama went and took a shower then came back and lay beside me. We talked about how fun it would be staying together, and she told me how thirsty Stretch was. I was a bit upset that Stretch tried to holla, but that shit was just in his nature.

We decided to get dressed so that we could go out and get something to eat. After getting dressed I headed out my room into the kitchen and noticed something that made my heart drop. Stretch was getting head on the couch, not only was he getting head it was from Midget's friend Alisha. This was completely against all code to bring one of my chicks friends to my house when I already have a bitch over here. After giving Stretch the I'ma kill you look he jumped up and put his dick in his pants. "Hey Shrimp," said Alisha.

I gave her a head nod, as Panama walked out my room I was nervous as shit. I just knew Alisha would blow my cover. "I was just leaving," said Alisha.

Panama stopped her and said, "Naw you ain't going anywhere, how the fuck you know Shrimp and Stretch?"

Alisha looked scared and said, "Shrimp fuck with my home girl Whitney, and I met Stretch over here through them a while back."

Before Panama could say anything I told Panama it ain't even like that. Panama walked back in the room and slammed the door. I instructed Alisha to leave and she told me she was telling Midget. "Tell her about the dick you was sucking too," I said as she stormed out.

I went in the room to see what Panama was doing and she was grabbing her belongings and getting ready to leave. She kept saying, "This ain't gonna work," as she was getting herself together.

Panama headed out my room and on the way to the front door. I put my back against the door and blocked her from leaving. I said, "That shit was old, why you trippin?"

Panama began to cry then pointed to Stretch and said, "Tell him Stretch. I can't do it. You gotta tell him."

Stretch looked at me, started laughing and said calmly, "I fucked her on the way here about four times in the car." Still with a smile on his face he shrugged his shoulders and said, "I had to put her to the test bro, and she failed."

I moved out the way and allowed Panama to walk out. Stretch walked up to me and says, "Just like old times man, she file and you always wifin em."

I didn't know if I should punch this nigga in the face or laugh. We dapped each other up and he left with Panama. I locked the door and went and sat on the couch. Tears began running down my face. *I couldn't win for losing. I keep chasing all these hoes and none of them are loyal.* I guess what I wanted in a girl was right there in North Carolina. My phone vibrated and I was hesitant to see who it was. I wasn't tryna hear from Stretch or Panama. I looked and I had two missed text messages.

Text Messages

2:15 pm Baby moms: *We miss you*

3:45 pm Bam: *Mcfluzie you still lovin these hoes Lmao.......*

191

The text from my baby mom's was uplifting but Bam brought me back to reality. As I'm reading the text a call comes through from Mr. Shutter. Anymore bad news and I'll have a mental breakdown. I answered trying to get my voice together, "Hello," I said.

Mr. Shutter says, "I got some news."

I grew quit clinching the couch and said, "Let me hear it."

Mr. Shutter then continued, "I have never seen this happen to one of my clients before, but after showing the sextape to the DA they believe that they have an even weaker case and agreed to drop the charges. Congratulations, use this as a lesson in life Christopher."

CHAPTER 20

MCFLUZIE

"Sometimes when you put all your eggs in one basket to better yourself it can come back and bite you."

After beating my case it was now time to make a change. My family was down in North Carolina and I think it was time for me to go home and get a fresh start. I had to make sure it was all out of my system though. I felt like I owed it to Midget to see her before I left, she did help bail me out and was there for me thru it all. Midget came over and it was awkward as all hell. Midget was in straight quarterback mode, she was throwing Tom Brady passes from all angles. I couldn't let this temptation overtake me.

As we sat in the living room and reminisced about the past I realized, I was really gonna miss her. Jeff and Blow was playing Madden while we were talking. After about an hour I told Midget that I was ready to hit the road. I stood up and gave her a big hug. I could hear Blow laughing his ass off as he seen Midget's feet dangling from off the ground. We held each other for about a good three minutes. I walked Midget to the door and before I could close it Blow said, "Aye one of my fantasies was always smashing a Midget, I'm always here."

We all started laughing but Blow and I knew he was dead ass. After I closed the door Blow had a grin on his face. He said, "You know you gotta put me on right?"

I ignored this nigga and headed to finish loading my stuff into the U-Haul truck. After I finished loading everything, I went back in to dapp Jeff and Blow up. I figured since I was gonna pass through Virginia I'd see my ex Temeaka. I have been talking to her back and forth for about a month and it seems she really does have her life together.

Temeaka didn't know when I was coming and that was exactly how I wanted it. On my way to Virginia I was on the phone with Bam and Stretch telling them how I changed my life. Bam and Stretch were good dudes but there was no way I could see them changing their heathen ways. Bam had stopped really gang banging and got a good job working at this store locking niggas up doing loss prevention. Now this Nigga Bam was supposed to be hard and anti-police, but he chasing niggas down and locking niggas up. If you asked Bam he says he only does it because he gets to fuck niggas up.

Now Stretch on the other hand went off to some historical black college to major in social studies. This nigga Stretch wanted to be a teacher. There was no way this nigga could graduate at 22 and avoid smashing 15-18 year Old's he would be teaching in High School, he was too thirsty. Through it all these were my boys and I love them. We started talking about Temeaka and I told them that I wanted to see her one last time to get some closure. These niggas insisted that I didn't do it because I would end up smashing.

At this point in my life I had self-control. I have been celibate for two and a half months and been studying the bible faithfully. When I make it back to North Carolina I had to lead by example. Bam said a lot has changed since I was last in VA Beach and started filling me in. He gave me the run down on the Clique. Biggs went off to school to play ball at Oregon for the Ducks and could go to the NFL. Chubs was still out the hood doing nothing. Thomas got 67 years, Squirrel got 59 years, and Snacks got 23 years for the string of things they did. Bam said Meech snitched on all of them and only did 6 months.

Bam then said, "And you gon like this."

I said, "Tell me," anxious to hear some more pillow talk.

Bam said, "You remember that blood nigga Big Keef that G checked you?"

I made an noise signaling him to continue.

"Well, he killed that bitch nigga Louis that knocked yo ass out."

My body began to tingle. I thought this was something that I would have liked but I wouldn't wish death upon my worst enemy. After getting myself together I asked Bam how he died. Bam then went on to say that Louis had ran in somebody house and robbed them and Big Keef was in there. He said that Louis apologized to Big Keef for pulling the gun out on him because it was dark and he didn't notice him.

Indo squashed everything and Louis thought everything was good. Bam said on the Fourth of July everyone was out the hood having a good time and Big Keef ran up on a Louis and shot him in the back of the head in the middle of the street. I didn't know what to say. Bam said, "And you wanna know the crazy thing Shrimp?"

I said, "What?"

Bam started laughing and said, "Nobody said a word. Big Keef still out here chillin."

It got silent for a second. Stretch broke the ice, "Well let me give you the update on the hoes." We all started laughing. Stretch then said, "Well Shrimp you know I go with Ericka so don't be trying nothing funny. I'm claiming her she off limits niggas."

I started laughing uncontrollably. After getting myself together, I said, "I hit that first like a hundred times."

We started laughing and then Bam said, "Nah remember I hit her first?"

Bam and I was dying laughing. I said while Bam continued to laugh, "This nigga liked to take my hoes and ends up wifin the biggest hoe of them all."

Stretch was furious. He said in a serious voice, "I guess Tameaka is a hoe too huh?" Everyone got silent again. "Tell him Bam," said Stretch.

"Tell me what?"

Bam started laughing and said, "I fucked Tameaka."

I couldn't even be mad, and on top of that I couldn't let these niggas know I was mad. Bam started to rub it in by saying, "Yeah, that bitch had some good pussy in High School and it's even better now."

I couldn't hold my anger in anymore. I said, "What you mean High School nigga?"

Bam said, "You ain't heard? I got her pregnant senior year and she had an abortion cause she ain't know if it was mine or some other niggas. Next thing I know you was wifin her."

I could have killed Bam. In complete anger I said, "That other Nigga was me pussy."

Bam and Stretch busted out laughing. I was mad as hell. After about five minutes of Stretch telling his story about me using rose pedals and him almost smashing at her house I had enough. I diverted the conversation back to Erica. "We all done smashed each other jumpoffs but at the end of the day u wifin Erica. Nigga that is your girl," I said.

Stretch tried to explain it saying that's when she was in High School and all that. He said him and Ericka got close when her brother got killed. I tried to act like I cared by asking questions because it seemed like he really cared for her. Stretch asked me did I remember when I was in the hospital and seen the news talking about having Thomas and Snacks in custody, and I told him I did. "Well they killed her brother in the woods out Oak Valley over drugs," he said.

It felt like my heart stopped beating. I was there that night. I witnessed the events leading up to it, I was the getaway driver. I changed the subject quick. I said, "Yo Bam what's good with yo cousin Rico?"

After no response I called his name a couple more times and no answer. "I think his call dropped," said Stretch.

I *knew why Bam hung up and this was something that we would just have to Take to the Grave.* I told Stretch I had to put my parents address in my GPS and I would call him back. *After I hung up I thought about how Bam said Meech was snitching, and if so why am I not in jail? These are answers I will never get or look for. I was gonna see Tameaka, but after what I just found out there was no use for me getting closure, I already had it.*

My past was now behind me. I'm starting a new life, I have a soon to be wife and a son waiting for me. I was anxious to get to North Carolina. I haven't spoken to my baby mom's or my son in a week. I had been so busy grinding getting ready for this big move. As I crossed the VA state lines I kept getting a call from a Baltimore number. I ignored it several times. The GPS said that I was five minutes away from my parents crib. My phone rang again with the Baltimore number and I answerd.

"Hey Shrimp," said the person on the other line, It was Keisha. "Don't ask me how I got your number. I realized that I can't live without you and I'm sorry for everything I put you through, I really wanna make this work."

I was shocked. Keisha was definitely wife material. I said, "I moved and I'm on my way to be with my baby mom's and son."

Keisha then began to talk about how she wants out of Baltimore and she wants to move with me for a fresh start. I didn't want her to keep blowing up my phone so I told her I would think about it and get back with her. After hanging up I thought to myself she a rider if she is willing to give up her life and come be a part of mine to study becoming a witness. As I pulled up to my parents crib I was shocked. Their house was crazy big. I wondered would my parent's ever forgive me if they knew all the things I was taking to the grave.

I parked the U-Haul truck and went to ring the doorbell. I just knew that my son would come running. Before I could ring the doorbell again my Mom opens the door. "Christopher, give your momma a kiss." I gave her a big hug and she kisses me on my cheek.

I saw my Dad in the living room on his laptop and I headed over to him. I patted his shoulder as I walked around him and said, "What's up Dad?"

My Dad tried to play the tuff role but broke quick. He stood up and gave me a hug, "Good to have you back son."

We sat down and started talking about how beautiful the house was and how much they like North Carolina. I said, "Where is Lashawn and Chris?"

My parents continued to talk about the house like I didn't just ask them a question. I asked them again in a louder tone. My Mom sat beside me and said with her hand on my back, "Lashawn took Chris and went to stay with her Aunt in Atlanta about three days ago. She said she was not ready to study becoming a witness and was still trying to find herself."

I stood up in anger and said out loud, "After all I done for her. I moved her here to a good place, bought her a car, helped her pay for school, sent her money and she just ups and leaves without saying a word to me?"

My mind started racing. *I gave up everything for a family with Laswawn and my son. I got rid of all my hoes, got my life in line with Jehovah, and I was really thinking about marriage with her. Is it the Devil working me or is Keisha a realistic idea? I leaned back on the couch with my hands over my face and all I could say was MCFLUZIE!!!!!!!!!!*

200

ACKNOWLEDGEMENTS

First off I would like to thank God. Through him all things are possible. I also would like to thank everyone who supported me on this project and helped me get thru this long process, you know who you are. I hope that this book was able to touch you as a reader and help you understand some of the things that people in this environment go thru. For those who are facing adversity like some of the characters in this book just know that there is light at the end of the tunnel.